FIELDS APART

J. N. KELLY

ISBN 978-1-64446-018-4

1 3 5 7 9 8 6 4 2

Printed in the United States of America
Published by

Rowe Publishing

www.rowepub.com

DEDICATION

For the neighborhood sandlot crew

CHAPTER

Millie Bauer leisurely peddled her powder blue bike up the driveway, her shoulder-length blond hair blowing in the breeze. Coasting around the back of the house, she leaned the two-wheeler against the weathered tannery shed and headed towards the back porch. Skipping past the empty birdbath, she hop-scotched the weeds on the path leading up to the house, needing just one of the three steps to make it onto the porch. It was the last day of school, and there was a spring in her step.

The house was silent. Millie was used to it now, but it bothered her every once in a while. It didn't help that there were all those pictures of people that weren't around anymore. She walked into the dining room and rolled the Pilot radio dial. The house filled with music as she passed by the front door. She sighed at the sight of no mail, peered through the mail slot, and then opened the door to make sure none had fallen back outside.

Millie ran upstairs to her bedroom to change into her tattered overalls. Actually, they were her brother, George's old pair, but he had outgrown those years ago. She grabbed her baseball mitt, also a hand-me-down, and stuffed her hair under a ball cap before rumbling back down the stairs.

The sound of big band music resonated throughout the house. Millie headed for the kitchen to make herself a peanut butter and jelly sandwich. She had only a few minutes to eat before she was to meet up with friends at Badger Park. Most of her classmates were heading over to Crescent Beach to swim, but Millie was able to round up enough players for a game of baseball. She hoped Paul Warren didn't show up, though. He always seemed to find a way to ruin the game.

It was an exciting time for Millie and her classmates. They were set to graduate from the eighth grade and move on to River Junction Central High School. Many people thought she was already in high school or even older, depending on what she was wearing. At 14 years old, Millie was the tallest in her class, at nearly six feet. She had always been the tallest in her class. Everyone in the Bauer family was tall. Millie, her mother, Helen, and brother, George, used to snicker when her father, Jim, ducked his 6'7" frame every time he came into a room.

The following morning the eighth graders were slated to receive their diplomas in a ceremony at the McAlpine State Theater. Then they were off to Lumbermen Park for the annual eighth grade Sawdust City Field Meet, where the class participated in a variety of athletic events. Millie was especially looking forward to the baseball toss.

Millie was washing down her last bite of sandwich with a glass of milk when there was a knock at the front door. She froze. Since the war had begun, unexpected knocks at the door got her heart racing.

"Come in," yelled Millie while the radio continued to blare.

No one entered the house.

"Come in," Millie shouted again. She turned down the radio and walked towards the front door, her heart pounding.

A few days ago, this happened, and it had been the Girl Scouts collecting lard.

"Come in," she called out one more time, hoping a familiar face entered.

Millie's hand shook, pulling aside the vestibule curtain. No one was there. She slowly opened the door. At her feet was a box with a big yellow ribbon. She knelt to pick up the parcel, her stomach fluttering. She quickly moved to the edge of the porch, looking down both ends of the street to see who had dropped it off. There was no one in sight.

"Hello?" she yelled, hopeful for a response.

No one did.

Millie returned to the house, the box rattling in her trembling hands. Her fear was changing to excitement. She moved into the dining room and set it in the middle of the table. She stared at the package for a few seconds, her blue eyes wide with curiosity. Finally, she carefully undid the ribbon, her hands still shaking.

Hovering over the now open box, Millie stared wide-eyed in amazement. It was exactly what she had been wishing for. It even looked like the one down at Buckley's Sporting Goods. She reached in and pulled

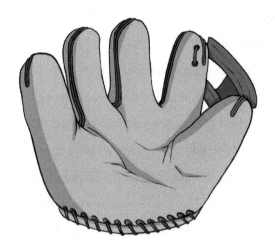

out a baseball mitt. It was the first new glove she had ever owned. For years she had used George's old one. She didn't mind but had pined for one of her own.

Millie slipped it onto her right hand. She held it up to her face and inhaled deeply, digging through the packing paper with her left hand, looking for some sort of sign of who sent it. At the bottom was a note that read: 'To Mox, one heck of a ballplayer. Have a great summer! Love, George. P.S. I'll be Home for Christmas.'

Goosebumps shot up and down Millie's arms. Did George actually write this note? It had to have been him. His nickname for her was "Mox," short for "Moxie." No one else called her that. Also, of late, George had been signing, "I'll be Home for Christmas," in hopes of it coming true. Since then, on most nights, Millie fell asleep to Bing Crosby crooning.

Christmas had been hard without George. From Millie's earliest memories, the holiday had been special for the family—baking cookies, singing carols, and lighting candle wreaths before midnight mass at St. Martin's Church. The last Christmas together as a family, they gathered around the radio listening to Lionel Barrymore as Ebenezer Scrooge in *A Christmas Carol*.

Millie double-checked the box for postal markings, but there were none. The note wasn't on the regular Victory-mail that she and George had been corresponding with for months, either. Millie didn't like the confinement of the standardized V-mail. Occasionally, she sent a four- or five-page letter in the regular mail, in addition to her monthly care package of chewing gum, cookies, candy bars, socks, soap, and newspaper clippings of what was going on around town.

Again, Millie sprinted upstairs to her room, retrieving George's letters from her father's tattered cigar box in the top drawer of her bureau. Neither Millie nor her mother had received anything from George in weeks. For a long time, they had each gotten a letter every couple of days, but that had stopped about a month ago—25 days to be exact. They didn't talk about it, but both were starting to worry.

Tears welled up in Millie's eyes when she compared signatures. She knew it was George's. The loop on the small "g" was exactly the same way.

Millie had to tell someone, but whom? Her mother wouldn't be getting home from the factory until after five o'clock. Maybe she could call Art Warren—Paul's brother. He was a close friend of George. Certainly, he would be excited to hear about the glove and maybe even know how George had gotten it to her.

Once again, Millie thundered downstairs towards the telephone. The clock read 3:50, and she was supposed to be at the park by four. She swiftly picked up the phone and began telling the operator to connect her to Warren's Grocery & Dry Goods number. Suddenly, another knock came at the front door.

Millie hung up the phone and hastily moved towards the door, still holding the new mitt.

"Maybe it's George," she said aloud, letting her imagination run wild.

With a large smile, Millie flung open the front door, but her grin quickly faded, and a chill ran up her spine. A telegram deliveryman stood in front of her.

The glove fell with a thud to the floor.

HELEN A BAUER

    636 PINE ST. RIVER JUNCTION

WISCONSIN=

THE SECRETARY OF WAR DESIRES ME TO

EXPRESS HIS DEEP REGRET THAT YOUR

SON PRIVATE FIRST CLASS GEORGE J BAUER

HAS BEEN REPORTED MISSING IN ACTION

SINCE MAY 5 IN ITALY. IF FURTHER DETAILS

OR OTHER INFORMATION ARE RECEIVED,

YOU WILL BE PROMPTLY NOTIFIED=

    M A SCHULTZ, ADJUNCT GENERAL

CHAPTER

O n December 8, 1941, the military recruiting station in downtown River Junction had a line wrapping around the block. It seemed like all over the city men were literally dropping what they were doing to enlist. Millie walked by one of the barbershops on her way home from school. On the door was a sign: "CLOSED! GONE TO WAR!" When she peeked inside, hair was strewn about the floor. It was as if the barber took a lunch break, decided to join up, and never bothered to come back to clean the shop.

A few nights later, the Bauer family silently huddled around the radio, listening to President Roosevelt's "Fireside Chat." His words echoed throughout the room:

We are now in this war. We are all in it—all the way.
Every single man, woman, and child is a partner in the
most tremendous undertaking of our American history.
We must share together the bad news and the good news,
the defeats and the victories—the changing fortunes
of war.

George spoke when their parents left the room.

"I'm going in the Army, Mox," he said with his back
to Millie.

Earlier in the day, she overheard him and Art talking
about George's favorite player, Bob Feller, enlisting in
the Navy.

"Do Mama and Pa know?" she asked.

"No, I just decided now," George replied, turning
to Millie, who was now facing away from him, fiddling
with the doily atop the radio.

Despite having half his senior year left at River
Junction Central High School, George was allowed
to enlist, receiving his diploma early. A dozen boys in
George's class joined the service, but it was his name
that made headlines in the *River Junction Review.*

The Friday before the Pearl Harbor attacks, George
announced that he was going to the University of

Wisconsin in Madison. He planned to study engineering and play football. It was front-page news in Sunday's edition of the *Review*. That was quickly forgotten when a second issue ran, highlighting what went on in Hawaii.

Pride filled Millie every time she was stopped on the street and asked about George, even from people she didn't know.

How's that brother of yours?

I'm sure George is showing them a thing or two over there!

George getting to play any ball over there?

When the family received letters from George, they gathered together, and her father read them aloud. Millie read the newspaper and listened to the radio to keep up with what was happening in the war. Her parents even put a world map up in the dining room next to the radio so they could visualize the progression of the conflict.

George was the only family member in uniform, but each member of the Bauer family did their part to support the war effort. They partook in bond drives and saved tin foil, newspaper, fats, and greases. Like President Roosevelt said, "We are all in it."

The Bauer's biggest contribution on the home front was the Victory Garden program that Millie's mother initiated in town. Victory Gardens sprang up all over the city: in back yards, vacant lots, even on a few building tops. A variety of fruits and vegetables were grown to help make up for food rationing and shortages. Beans, beets, cabbage, carrots, kale, kohlrabi, lettuce, peas, tomatoes, turnips, and squash were grown in abundance. What wasn't consumed was canned for use at a later date. Mrs. Bauer even wrote a weekly column for the *Review* for the best ways to manage your garden.

In August 1942, everything changed when Mr. Bauer was killed.

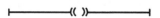

It was sunset as Millie and her parents were returning from Timber Point. Mrs. Bauer had just won a blue ribbon for her strawberry jam at the Western Wisconsin District Fair. The family happily chatted, their yellow Chevy pickup kicking up dust on the back roads between Timber Point and River Junction.

As the truck bounced along the uneven country terrain, they came upon a tractor on the side of the road. The owner was drenched in sweat and covered in dirt, trying to fix a tire.

Millie's father pulled the truck up behind the tractor. "Millie, why don't you grab the toolbox and give us a hand," instructed her father.

The Bauers lived on a farm until Millie was six, so Jim Bauer had changed dozens of tractor tires. "I could change a tire in my sleep during a blizzard," he used to brag. This always made Millie laugh. She thought one or the other would have been impressive enough.

Millie and her father hopped out of the truck, walking along the waving Indian grass.

"Don't forget the toolbox," shouted Mrs. Bauer from the cab. Millie had been so excited that she ran towards the tractor, forgetting the tools altogether. Her forgetfulness saved her life.

"Why don't you get that, Mildred?" motioned her father towards the bed of the truck. "I'm going to see what we're dealing with."

Those were the last words she heard him speak.

As Millie jumped out of the bed, she heard what sounded like a gunshot. When she came around the truck, she saw her father and the farmer had been blown into the ditch by an exploding tire.

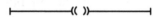

The days and weeks that followed were a blur. Millie knew that her father was well-liked, but she quickly lost count of the people that came and went from the Bauer home. The one person she had hoped to see—George— never walked through the door. Even moments before her father's funeral at an overflowing St. Martin's Church, Millie held out hope that George would emerge from the congregation. Millie and her mother found out afterward that George did not receive the message of his father's tragic death until several weeks later. They mourned together through letters.

Shortly after her father's passing, Millie's mother quit her waitressing job and went to work full-time at the River Junction Ordinance Plant, making ammunition for the war. She aged overnight. Gray overtook her chestnut hair, and wrinkles creased her face. She worked eight hours a day, six days a week at the plant. On Sunday, her one day off, she and Millie went to church in the morning and then found somewhere to volunteer.

Millie consistently read the newspaper. She learned to fear names like Benito Mussolini and Joseph Stalin. The person she feared the most was Adolph Hitler, the leader of Nazi Germany. Mr. Bauer had always spoken proudly of being a farmer of German heritage. "After all," he would say. "'Bauer' is the German word for 'farmer.'" When Millie read about what Hitler was doing, she was ashamed.

Mrs. Bauer spent her weekday evenings at the local Armory. She worked in the kitchen, feeding the soldiers who were training. She then went over to the adjacent barracks, tending to soldiers that had come home injured.

"I see a lot of boys like George in those infirmary beds," Mrs. Bauer said one night when she arrived home exhausted.

CHAPTER

Millie never ventured over to Badger Park. She barely made it up to her room. She crawled into bed, clutching the telegram in one hand and cradling her new glove in the other. She read the telegram dozens of times, hoping that the words would somehow change to good news. When it didn't, she folded it as many times as she could and buried it deep into her overalls pocket.

The appearance of the telegram delivery man was a shock to Millie. She had thought about what she would say or do if one came to the door. At least it wasn't a soldier. A soldier at your door meant someone had died. She will never be able to erase the memory of passing Mrs. Benson's house. She was putting laundry on the line in her backyard when two men in Army uniforms arrived. The thought of her blood-curdling scream made Millie want to scream, too.

Millie stood mutely when the man handed her the telegram. She had no idea who he was, and they never made eye contact. Western Union hired men from surrounding towns to do these types of deliveries.

Millie sat up in bed and stared out the window at the tannery shed in the backyard. It hadn't been used in a few years. The summer her father had died, to be exact. He built it for her mother to store canned goods, but George got the most use out of it.

Mr. Bauer painted a squatting catcher on the back of the shed in the likeness of Chicago Cubs catcher Gabby Hartnett, a favorite of his and George. A home plate was placed into the ground in front of the catcher, and a pitcher's mound was constructed 60'6" away. George spent hours out there throwing a ball to either his father or the two-dimensional Hartnett. Millie could still hear him heaving ball after ball against the shed wall.

Whack! Whack!

The catcher's paint was now cracked and faded, and weeds had overgrown the pitcher's mound.

Millie's daydream was broken by a noise downstairs.

"Mother," she mouthed.

"Millie," shouted her mother from downstairs. "Millie, are you home, dear?"

Millie heard her mother climbing the stairs, each step squeaking louder than the last. Quickly, Millie decided she wouldn't tell her about either of the deliveries. As the footsteps approached her room, Millie hurriedly stuffed the glove under her bed and felt for the telegram in her pocket. She rolled over, her back to the door, feigning sleep.

Millie's mother gently knocked on the door and opened it a crack. "Millie?"

Millie squeezed her eyes tightly. Her mother sat down next to her. "Is everything all right, Mildred?" she inquired in a concerned tone. "The front door was wide open, and the radio was on."

Millie rolled over and put on her best groggy face. "I'm just not feeling well, mama," she said.

Millie's mother put the back of her hand to her daughter's head and then her cheeks.

"When did this start?" Mrs. Bauer's once vibrant, green eyes now were tired.

"When I got home from school," said Millie, continuing the lie.

"I walked by Badger Park on the way home, and all the boys were wondering where you were," said her mother, moving closer to Millie on the bed.

"They were?" replied Millie in a voice that didn't match her supposed illness. She was tempted to say she felt better so that she could run over to the park to join them, but her mother quelled that thought.

"Say, Millie, what is that package on the dining room table?" inquired her mother.

"It was from George," blurted out Millie, having forgotten to do something with the package.

"From George?" said her mother, stammering and rising to her feet. "What...what was it?"

Millie reached under her bed, grabbed the new mitt, and handed it to her mother.

"Oh, Millie, what a dandy," said her mother holding the mitt in her hands and blinking rapidly to hold back tears. "Did he...did he send a note?"

Millie could only point over to her dresser where the brief correspondence lay.

Millie's mother walked over and read the last sentence aloud. Her voice quivered as she read, "I'll be home for Christmas." She had tears in her eyes and a smile on her face.

"Let's hope he's home sooner than Christmas," she said, taking a deep breath. She walked over and kissed Millie on the forehead. "Is there anything I can get for you before I head over to the Armory?"

Still tight-lipped, Millie shook her head no, avoiding her mother's caring eyes. She put her hand in her pocket to make sure the telegram was still there.

"Would you like me to stay home, Millie?" asked her mother, grabbing Millie's chin and raising it up so their eyes met. Her mother's eyes, still glistening, were much brighter than when she came into the room.

Once again, Millie shook her head no.

"All right then, dear, I'm leaving. I'll be home around ten." She bent down and gave Millie one final kiss on the forehead. "You try to get some rest. You have a big day tomorrow," she added before leaving the room.

Millie waited until her mother left and then went next door into George's bedroom. Not much had changed since he left for basic training in Little Rock,

Arkansas, shortly after his enlistment in January 1942. His heavy white letterman's sweater with the large red "RJ" still hung over the chair at his desk. Balsa wood model airplanes dangled from the ceiling. Pictures of his favorite athletes, torn out of magazines, were taped to the walls, with a shrine to Bob Feller matted above his bed. Millie spotted what she was looking for—George's newspaper article scrapbook. Millie grabbed the large red book off his dresser and headed back to her room.

Sprawled out on her bed, Millie haphazardly looked through the bulging scrapbook, trying to distract herself. There was every newspaper article that mentioned George dating back to when he was eight years old and won a foot race at Pioneer Days Festival. There were more and more as he got older, and by the time he was a junior in high school, they could have run a weekly column in the *Review* on all of his accomplishments. It didn't matter what the sport was, George was always the star.

Shortly after sunset, Millie fell into a surprisingly deep sleep with the scrapbook still splayed open next to her. Bing Crosby sang her to sleep.

CHAPTER

The smell of bacon wafted up from the kitchen into Millie's room. She quickly put on her red and white polka dot graduation dress, placing the telegram in the front pocket.

"Are you excited for today, dear?" asked her mother as Millie entered the kitchen, still blurry-eyed.

"Yes," said Millie trying to sound excited. She reached into her dress pocket, feeling for the telegram.

"I'm hoping that I can make it over to graduation," said her mother, moving from the icebox to the stove.

"I hope so, too," Millie replied anxiously.

"Say, can you go grab the newspaper for me, please, Millie," asked her mother.

Every Monday and Thursday, the *Review* ran a roster of "Missing in Action" and "Killed in Action" soldiers from the state of Wisconsin. Local names were in bold print.

Filled with dread, Millie scurried to the front porch. She fumbled with the paper on the steps until she found the listing. A quick scan saw George wasn't listed. For an instant, she contemplated telling her mother about the telegram that was burning a hole in her pocket. But, when she got back into the house, her mother had turned the radio on and was waltzing around the kitchen as she served breakfast.

"Your favorite, dear—bacon, eggs, and a side of apples with honey," said Millie's mother with a smile.

"Thank you," said a famished—and relieved—Millie.

"Now eat up, dear," said her mother, taking the paper and guiding Millie over to the table. "You have a big day ahead of you."

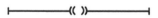

Back row; middle. That's where Millie knew she was supposed to stand—that's where she always was. One last picture before graduation. She stood quietly as her teacher, Mrs. Glass, tried to assemble the class around her for the picture. In her left hand, Millie clutched the telegram, now folded into 16 squares. She hadn't let it out of her sights the entire night or morning. She stuffed it back into the left pocket of her dress.

Millie's classmates giddily argued over who was going to win the events at the meet. She was in no mood to. It didn't matter anyways. She didn't really have any friends in her class to speak to. She got along okay with some of the boys—most of whom she played ball with whenever possible. Plus, she didn't care for the things that girls in her class did. She'd rather look at comics or play marbles and jacks with the guys at recess. Most of all, she liked to talk baseball.

Guilt balled up inside of her thinking about George—wherever he was—and then her unknowing mother at the factory working. Whatever exciting plans she had for the summer were squelched by yesterday's delivery.

"Are any of you going to the free movie next week at Delta Cinema?" asked a loud raspy voice to the left of Millie, distinguishing itself above the dull roar. "At least it's free if you sold enough bonds."

Millie didn't have to look over to know that it was Paul Warren. There had been a time when Millie and Paul were friendly, but then Millie hit her growth spurt. On the other hand, Paul had grown out rather than up. He had been cold to Millie since, taking every opportunity he could to belittle her.

Paul was dressed in his khaki green Boy Scout uniform, red hair flickering in the sun. He looked straight out of a Norman Rockwell painting. Millie figured that's probably why he was so successful at selling bonds. He was a Four Freedoms poster come to life.

Paul was talking to students from other schools. He, too, had few, if any, friends among his classmates.

"Even if you have to pay, you should come because 50 percent of the door sales are being donated to the Boy Scouts," he continued, straightening his red neckerchief. "Oh yeah, and I'll be getting a service badge for selling the most war bonds."

Millie could almost hear Paul's smirk and nostrils flaring.

"Do you get the *Review* where you live," he asked, dominating the conversation. "Yesterday, there was an article about me selling the most bonds of any scout."

The group slowly began distancing themselves from him, but he babbled on.

"I hear that they are going to show *Where Do We Go from Here?* But as the top seller, I'm going to try to talk them into showing *Pride of the Yankees*," he added.

Paul caught Millie's eye with mention of the Lou Gehrig movie. Baseball was the one thing they could still converse about.

Millie was just about to say she'd go when Mrs. Glass broke in.

"I want my eighth graders to get lined up for one last photograph before we head into the theater," she said in her customary stern tone.

It took just a few minutes, and soon Millie's class was filing into the dimly lit McAlpine State Theater. All of the eighth graders from River Junction and surrounding towns such as Timber Point and Porter Lake were there. The gaggle produced a dull rumble of noise.

Millie's class was seated near the back of the auditorium and soon added to the clamoring when a booming voice came over the loudspeaker. "Attention, eighth graders! Attention, eighth graders!" The amplified voice of Junior High Principal, Mr. Hall, crackled through the public address system. "We will be beginning the ceremony momentarily," he shouted. His attempts to be heard went unmet.

Suddenly, a crisp whistle pierced the commotion. Millie immediately knew who it was. She looked around and saw Coach Shellman briskly walking toward the stage. He had his pinkies in the corners of his mouth, emitting the shrill sound. He leapt on stage, bypassing the stairs. Most of the boys quieted down when they saw it was coach, except for a few gasps at the athletic feat. The girls ceased talking at the urging of the boys.

Coach Shellman was the physical education teacher at River Junction Central High School and coach for the school's football, basketball, and baseball teams. He coached George and had been in the Bauer home numerous times over the years. While he was known for his gruff persona, Millie had seen a side of him that others rarely did. He was a pallbearer at her father's funeral in place of George. Ever since then, he looked out for Millie and her mother, whether it be fixing a leaky faucet or dropping off some dinner for Millie when her mother was working late.

"All right, eighth graders, you aren't in high school yet," barked coach.

The theater remained silent except for the hum of the P.A. system.

"Remember, you can always repeat eighth grade," he continued. "Then you'll be really good at this next year."

"And one more thing," he added. "For all of you who don't think you are getting a diploma, and your name is called—don't ask any questions."

Coach's mouth broke into a half-smile, revealing some of his tobacco-stained teeth.

"If I see any of you dillydallying, you won't be a part of the Meet. You won't be sitting on the sideline, either. You'll be weeding the football field," he said, mimicking a raking motion.

A few boys laughed because they thought they were supposed to. "We'll see who's laughing," he added, once again silencing the crowd.

While almost everyone sat glued to their chair, intimidated even to move, Millie covered a knowing smile with her hand. She knew that coach took sports very seriously but little else.

Millie wasn't surprised at how quiet everyone around her was. For weeks, participation in the City Meet had been used as a threat by Mrs. Glass. Every minor infraction brought about a promise of having to sit out if the behavior continued. Most of the boys were on their best behavior because Coach Shellman often used the Meet as one of his ways to start measuring their athletic talent long before they got into high school.

"Thank you, coach," coughed Principal Hall, embarrassed at the ease of Coach Shellman's crowd control skills.

"As I was saying, I just have to give you a few instructions, and remember, the faster we get done here, the faster you will get over to Lumbermen Park for the Meet." Principal Hall smiled, giving a slight bow towards coach, now standing off to the side of the stage.

Millie stopped listening to Principal Hall's instructions. They were the same that Mrs. Glass had been repeating for weeks. "Calmly walk across the stage. Reach with your left hand and shake with your right."

They had even practiced it. It was too late if someone didn't understand by now.

The lights were turned off, except for on stage. Millie fidgeted in her chair as her eyes adjusted to the darkened theater. She waited for her class to be called. One by one, names were read. Each walked across the large theater stage, flawlessly shook Principal Hall's hand, and received a diploma.

A girl named Gretel Farnsworth echoed through the theater. The bubbly brunette bounced across the stage. Millie didn't know her. She didn't know any of the students thus far.

Millie craned her neck to count the rows before her class was to go. She counted four. In just a matter of minutes, she would be done with eighth grade and on to high school. Her eyes wandered behind her when a person caught her eye. Sitting in the last row, she thought she saw the silhouette of her mother. Even though her eyes had adjusted to the now dark theater, she squinted to get a better look.

"Eyes forward, Mildred," said Mrs. Glass, suddenly at Millie's side.

"Yes, Mrs. Glass," replied Millie obediently, slinking back into her seat.

It seemed like forever for the four rows to make their way to the stage, but now it was Millie's turn. Once she was positioned to make her way up the stairs, she tried to look back into the audience to see her mother, but the stage lights made everyone in the back of the darkened theater indistinguishable.

"Mildred Bauer," her name echoed around the theater.

Millie felt for the telegram before carefully climbing the stairs. Her stomach lurched as she made her way across the stage. She reached for the diploma with her right hand and shook with her left, eliciting laughter in the crowd. She could feel her face go flush from embarrassment walking off stage.

CHAPTER

Millie and her classmates sat quietly in the shade of Lumbermen Park's grandstand, nervously awaiting instructions from Coach Shellman. For a moment, she was able to look beyond the turmoil of the last 24 hours. She gazed out across the well-manicured baseball diamond. Lumbermen Park had always been special to Millie's family. It was the reason they moved to River Junction.

The Bauer farm was east of River Junction. It was one of several in the county that didn't survive the Depression. Millie's father landed a job as a bricklayer in 1934 to help build Lumbermen Park's football and baseball fields as part of President Roosevelt's New Deal.

They moved to River Junction in 1937, the spring the baseball field opened. Millie was at the first game, a 7-5 River Junction Rafters loss to the Superior Lakers. She sat on her father's shoulders as the workers were honored at the dedication ceremony during the park's first-night baseball game that June. Since then, Millie had spent numerous days and evenings at the park watching the Rafters with George, the Warren boys, and whoever else wanted to tag along.

There hadn't been much baseball at Lumbermen Park the past couple of years. The North Country League, which the Rafters were a member of, had canceled the last two seasons, and there were no plans to reconvene in 1944. River Junction Central High School still played there, and the River Junction County League had a few exhibition games.

Lumbermen Park was the scene of numerous athletic conquests by George. He scored touchdowns five different ways against Cedar Point, pitched a no-hitter against Falling Ax, and swept the sprints in a track meet, to name a few.

After hitting a pair of home runs, including a game-winner in another game against Cedar Point, the *Review* wrote: "If George Bauer keeps this up, they'll build a statue of him and rename Lumbermen Park, 'George Bauer Stadium.'"

Once again, Paul Warren's raspy voice pierced the chatter of the crowd and Millie's thoughts. "Hey, Bauer, you forget which is your left and which is your right?" he said loudly while sitting down next to her. A few people laughed. Millie tried to ignore him.

Paul had also spent a lot of time at Lumbermen Park watching games with his brothers and the Bauer siblings. They were all members of the Rafters Knothole Gang, a group of kids who got into games for a nickel.

To say the Knothole Gang watched the games was misleading. Often times they were playing a game beyond the left field fence while the Rafters game was going on. Sometimes, The Knotinghole Gang's ball would sail over the fence onto the Lumbermen Park playing field, halting play. They were never told to stop, though. Once in a while, the *Review* would write a gag article about the Knothole Gang's game when the Rafters lost big.

"What events did you sign-up for?" Paul asked. Each student was allowed to participate in anywhere from four to six of the events: high jump, broad jump, long jump, chin-up bar, relay race, 50-yard dash, shuttle race, jump rope, and baseball throw.

Before Millie could answer, Paul replied to his own question with an air of confidence. "I figured I would save all of my energy for the baseball toss," he said smugly, much to the annoyance of Millie. "I'm also signed up for jump rope, chin-up bar, broad jump, and shuttle run."

The baseball toss was the most coveted event to win and was always the last of the day. All the kids came together and got one throw.

Paul was oblivious to the fact that he was just not a good athlete. No matter what sport he tried, he was too small and slow. If there was one thing that Paul could do well on the baseball diamond, though, it was catch. He was adept at receiving Millie's unique pitching delivery. This dated back to when they were little and often not allowed to play games with the older kids, so they would play on the side. It quickly became established that Millie was pitcher and Paul, catcher.

Millie grew up playing both baseball and softball. From that, she developed a hybrid pitching release, submarine style. In addition, she was left-handed, making the ball naturally dart and dive depending on how she gripped it. "You throwing a spitball at me, lefty?" her father would tease after having to chase down a pitch that eluded his glove at the last second.

Millie shared the same strategy with Paul for the meet, but not because she thought she was going to win the baseball toss. She was more concerned with hurting herself or someone else. When she really cut loose running or jumping, it was a flurry of arms and legs. When she tossed a baseball, it was the same flailing of limbs, but she was confident— she always had been. Her father liked to say, "Millie, you could throw before you could walk—and you're still better at the former than the latter."

Millie hemmed and hawed, knowing that if Paul was aware she had the same plans, he would loudly accuse her of copying him. He would probably go tell Coach Shellman that she was going to lollygag through the other events to have an advantage at the baseball toss, even though that was his plan.

Before Millie could respond, the crowd's attention was suddenly turned to the group striding onto the field. Coach Shellman was flanked by five athletes from Central High. The only one that Millie recognized was Walter Edwards. The *River Junction Review* often referred to him as the "heir apparent" to George.

Coach tended to have his favorite athletes help him during Meet Day. This gave him free rein to roam around, watching as many students as he wanted. Afterward, his players gave input on someone he may have missed. George had done this a few years in a row.

The group was still about 100 feet away when coach began blowing the whistle around his neck and hollering out orders. "I want girls lined up on the third baseline and boys down first," he shouted, giving a shrill, extended blow of the whistle.

The eighth graders sprung up from where they were seated and scrambled towards their respective sides of the ball diamond. Millie loped to a spot halfway between home plate and third base. When they were situated, a few of the Central High athletes counted them off by fives. Millie ended up being a "one" and seemed to be the only girl that wasn't swooning over the high school boys. She was too concerned with what number Paul was to pay attention to them.

Paul was easy to see in his Boy Scout uniform and flickering red hair, but Millie kept losing count when the boys around Paul got out of line, trying to figure out who else was in their group. She just hoped he wasn't in hers.

"Ones on the pitcher's mound, twos at home plate, threes at first base, fours at second base, and fives at third," Coach ordered from home plate. "When you get there, your group leader will explain everything to you."

Millie kept her eyes on Paul as they both approached the mound. "Please walk by and go to third, please walk by and go to third," she said under her breath. Paul remained on the opposite side of the mound glaring across at her. The group crowded around Walter Edwards, listening to his directions.

Millie moved from station to station under the hot midday sun. Both she and Paul kept tabs on one another to ensure the other was at least appearing to give their best effort. When Coach Shellman happened to walk by with his notepad, Millie intensified the look on her face. Otherwise, she gave minimal effort. Her mind wandering to the telegram in her overalls pocket, she began losing enthusiasm for the baseball toss.

Finally, coach blew his whistle, and everyone lined up at home plate for the big toss. As a "one," Millie was at the front of the line. She soon found everyone lining up behind her, making her the first one to go. Off to the side, coach stood talking to Mr. Christopher, the *Review's* sportswriter, who always penned a feature on the meet. Next to them was Walter Edwards, holding a clipboard to keep track of the distances.

As Millie waited for everyone to file in, she watched the high school athletes mark off the feet by 25 with a yardstick stuck in the ground. They started at 50 and worked up to 225—"The Bauer Mark," as it had come to be known in recent years. Of what Millie knew, no one had ever thrown it past 200 feet, except for George, who reached the mythical 225 mark.

"All right," bellowed coach, once everyone was in somewhat of a line. "I want you to say your name to Edwards before you throw. Once you are done, you are free to leave. If you want to stick around and watch, don't get in the way—and no dillydallying."

Millie had already decided that she would do her toss and then head home. She was in no mood to watch everyone throw.

"One last thing before you toss," said coach, now striding back and forth in front of the antsy children. "Playground starts on June 12th. I expect to see all of you out at the parks during the summer. I don't care if you are weaving baskets or shooting baskets; I want to see you there."

Coach blew his whistle and handed the ball to Millie. "Let's see that Bauer arm," he murmured out of the side of his mouth.

Once the ball was in her hand, Millie became energized. "Millie Bauer," she said to Walter Edwards, who gave her a smile and nodded encouragingly, "Got get 'em, Little Bauer."

Millie took a deep breath, got a running start, and threw the ball with all of her might. It left her hand in a perfect arc, rising into the blue sky.

The high school boys at the 225 feet mark jumped to their feet and got out of the way right as the ball struck the yardstick, knocking it to the ground.

A few of the boys behind Millie murmured. She heard Mr. Christopher whistle in amazement. "You see that, Shell," he said, elbowing Coach Shellman in his excitable, squeaky voice.

"I think we found ourselves a winner," coach responded just loud enough for Millie, Mr. Christopher, and Walter Edwards to hear.

"227," shouted the boy who had to dive to get out of the way.

"Well, I'll be," said coach shaking his head in disbelief.

CHAPTER  6

Creaking steps awoke Millie. Before she could turn her back, her mother was at the bedroom door with a newspaper in hand. Millie's heart jumped at the sight, but her mother's smiling face quickly put her at ease.

"I'm sorry to wake you, dear, but I wanted you to see this before I left for the barracks," said Mrs. Bauer holding up the morning edition of the *Review*.

Millie sat up in bed. Her mother handed her the paper and sat down on the end of the bed.

Wiping the sleep from her eyes, Millie let out a yelp. "What the?" she said, looking at her mother and then back at the newspaper wide-eyed.

Millie was looking at a cartoon of herself at the Field Meet. The caricature was of her throwing a baseball to the sun. The Caption read: "Bauer out throws 'em all!"

Millie was speechless.

Mrs. Bauer leaned over and hugged her daughter. "I'm so proud of you, my dear," she said. "And I know both your father and brother would be, too."

The mention of her father and brother brought a wave of sorrow. Millie wished they were there to share in the moment.

"What do you think father would say if he could see this?" Millie asked with a twinge of sadness.

The question brought a smile and a rare twinkle to her mother's tired eyes. "Something to make us laugh," she said, biting her lower lip.

Mr. Bauer always had something funny to say whenever George's picture was in the paper. He would act unimpressed, taking interest in another mundane article, which drove his son crazy.

"I'll leave some money on the dining room table," said Mrs. Bauer. "Why don't you head down to Truman's later this morning and pick up a few copies of the *Review*?"

Millie forced a smile and nodded.

"And make sure to get one for your brother," added her mother.

"Yes, mother," responded Millie.

"Looks like we'll have to get a scrapbook started for you," said a beaming Ms. Bauer.

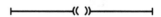

Millie tried in vain to get back to sleep but, alas, could not. She got up, put on her familiar overalls, pocketed the telegram, and walked a few blocks over to Truman's Grocery. With the best penny candy selection in the neighborhood, the small corner store attached to the Truman house was a familiar stop for Millie and George when they came across some spare change.

"Well, well," said Mr. Truman, looking over the top of his glasses at Millie as she entered the shop. He held up the picture of Millie in the paper.

Millie could feel herself blushing.

"I guess I'll have to start calling it the *Daily Bauer Update* again," Mr. Truman said with a smile. He always kept aside a few copies when George's name appeared in it—which was often. He set down a stack of the *Review* in front of Millie.

"Thank you so much, Mr. Truman," said Millie gratefully. "How much do I owe you?"

"How about sending me some tickets when you are pitching for the Cubs?" he said, handing over the newspapers.

"It's a promise," responded Millie with a laugh.

"Just to sweeten the deal, how about you grab a handful of penny candies?" Mr. Truman said, motioning to the wall of wicker baskets brimming with treats: jawbreakers, licorice, taffy, bubble gum, candy corn, and bottle caps.

Millie's eyes got big. With a smile, she plunged her free hand into the wicker basket of taffy. Mr. Truman smiled again and nodded before being summoned to the deli by another customer.

"Tell your mother I said hello," he called after Millie as she was leaving the building.

"I will, and thank you again, Mr. Truman," she replied, turning around with a wave.

Millie walked outside with her stack of papers and pocket full of taffy. She didn't notice the Green Dodge that was pulling up to the curb. The blaring horn made her jump.

"Millie," shouted Art Warren from behind the wheel.

"Hi, Art," replied Millie with a breathless laugh, embarrassed to have walked right past him. "What are you up to?"

"Just got done with morning deliveries," he said. He playfully pointed at the four newspapers in her hand. "Say, you gonna read all of those?"

Millie bashfully smiled and shook her head, "No."

"Hop in; I'll give you a ride," said Art, reaching across the front seat and opening the passenger side door. He slid his white letterman sweater and red ball cap over to make room for Millie. She stepped off the curb up into the truck's cab.

Millie always liked Art. He had been friends with George since the Bauers moved to River Junction. Like George, Art was an outstanding athlete, but during the summer between ninth and 10th grade, he contracted polio while on a trip to Milwaukee. Showing symptoms shortly after arriving back home, he was quarantined his entire sophomore year. When he returned to school, he had a pronounced limp that made playing sports impossible. However, he happily stayed involved as team manager.

"So, what's with all the papers there, Millie?" asked Art with a smile.

Millie opened the paper, exposing her picture and holding it up, so Art could look at it while he drove.

"Bauer out throws 'em all," he read aloud, grabbing the newspaper out of her hand. "Well, hot dog, Millie," Art said, slapping his knee excitedly.

"Thanks, Art," said Millie, flattered by his reaction.

"Bauer out throws 'em all," he repeated, shaking his head and laughing. "Hot dog!"

The pair rode for a few blocks in silence. Millie basked in the glow of Art's praise. Then, suddenly, he began laughing.

"What's so funny?" Millie self-consciously asked. Maybe there was ink on her nose from the newspapers. She tried to remember if she had touched her face.

"Oh, it's just that Paul told me that you only outthrew him by a few feet," replied Art, trying to catch his breath.

Millie laughed heartily for the first time in a few days, releasing the tension that had been building since the telegram arrived. For a moment, she forgot her burden, imagining Paul fibbing. It was good to have tears of laughter fall down her cheeks.

After the cackling subsided, Millie causally asked Art about her brother. "So, have you gotten any letters from George lately?"

"Nah, the last I heard from him was about a month ago," replied Art with a twinge of disappointment. "He was wondering how the Indians were doing without Feller."

Millie sighed, looking out the window as they pulled onto her street. She wondered if Art would keep her secret.

"How 'bout you?" asked Art curiously.

"27 days since his last letter," responded Millie.

"Not that anyone's counting," joked Art, giving Millie a nudge. "Well, maybe your baseball toss will make some European newspapers and get him to write you a letter."

Millie laughed and shook her head as they pulled into the driveway. She'd forgotten how funny Art was. She wondered how he and Paul could be brothers.

"You could always just throw one of the papers over to him," continued Art on his ribbing.

"Maybe I'll ask Paul to," retorted Millie, climbing out of the truck. "Thanks for the ride, Art. See you around."

"I'll tell him to get his arm loosened up," replied Art, slapping the door and waving as he pulled out of the driveway.

"The glove," Millie said aloud. Amidst all the excitement and trying to conceal the telegram, she had forgotten to mention her new prized possession.

"Art!" Millie shouted after him, but he had already turned the corner.

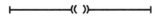

A couple of days later, Millie's mother was once again at the foot of her bed with a newspaper in hand.

"Ugh, another article about me?" Millie playfully said. "Well, I did eat a ham sandwich yesterday."

Mrs. Bauer didn't return the kittenish tone. She showed Millie the headline about the Normandy Invasion.

"I hope George is all right," said Mrs. Bauer, her voice wavering.

"Me, too," replied Millie, swallowing hard.

CHAPTER

Millie rarely left the house over the next few days. When she wasn't scouring the *Review* for word of George, she stayed within earshot of the radio, peeking out the window for the mailman, or, heaven forbid, the return of the telegram deliveryman. In between, she unfolded the telegram and obsessively read it. Her momentary feeling of pride from the Field Meet triumph had quickly dissipated when she saw what was taking place over in France.

Noticing Millie's frantic state, her mother stopped the newspaper subscription. If Millie wanted to read it, she would have to go to the library.

"If there is anything about you in the *Review*, we'll be sure to go buy one," said Millie's mother playfully.

"Mother," Millie responded with a chortle.

"Why don't you go and find a ball game, Millie?" prodded her mother, practically pushing her daughter towards the door. "I'm sure Paul and the gang are out and about."

Millie hadn't talked to any of the boys that she usually played with, but she was sure that there was a game going on at one of the sandlots. She hopped on her bike, put her new glove on the handlebar, and headed out in search of a game.

It didn't take long before Millie came upon a group at the third ward diamond. Surrounded by woods that gave the feeling of a stadium, it was one of her favorite places to play in the city. The makeshift backstop was made of chicken wire. Well-worn grass patches marked the bases. There was no outfield fence, but in left field stood the legendary stable.

Over 400 feet of dry, yellowed grass stood between home plate and the worn livery that leaned whichever way the wind was blowing. A dirt road ran alongside the lot and into the woods. No kid had ever hit one over it, but George swore he saw Pete Dowling, who played for the River Junction Rafters, hit one over when he was messing around with some of the neighborhood kids.

Millie didn't recognize any of the boys until she heard Paul Warren's familiar voice.

"Oh great, here comes Olive Oyl," he sarcastically called out. The boys turned their attention to Millie.

Millie could feel herself starting to blush. She hadn't seen Paul behind the others. If she had, she would have gone the other way. She was too close now, though.

"Hey, wanna play?" said a wiry dark-haired boy in a red St. Louis Cardinals cap

Paul nudged him and scowled.

"What?" said the boy, "We only have seven."

"Fine, but she's on your team, Ted," said Paul.

"All right with me," said Ted with a shrug. He smiled and nodded in Millie's direction. "Weren't you just talking to us about that throw she had yesterday?"

"Hold on," piped up one of Paul's soon-to-be teammates. "We want her."

"Yeah, you can have Paul," said another snickering.

"You guys know who George Bauer is?" asked Paul, ignoring the negotiations. He then went into a longwinded tale of the time George stole second, third, and home in one inning against Timber Point.

Millie was confused. George had been Paul's hero, but he continued to torment her. She wondered how Paul would take the news about George. Guilt began to ball up inside her. *Was it okay that she was keeping the news from all these people that loved and admired George?*

"Save it, Paul," said Ted, cutting him off. "Let's play."

Another boy, also wearing a worn St. Louis Cardinals cap, who looked just like Ted, but a few years younger, piped in, "We get last ups!"

"Suit yourselves, boys," said Paul. He tossed the ball at Millie's feet.

"Wow, that is a beaut," said one of the other boys with a whistle, noticing Millie's glove.

The others crowded around to admire the mitt. Even Paul was impressed. "Where did you get that?" he enviously asked.

"George gave it to me," said Millie proudly.

Ted tossed the ball towards Millie. "If you're anything like your brother, I guess you should pitch."

Millie smiled. She caught the ball and headed for the grassless area that was the pitcher's mound.

"You're Ted?" asked Millie as the boy ran by her.

He stopped and fidgeted with his hat. "Yup, and that's my brother, Phil, and my buddy, Tim. We are members of the Scouts Troop 13 in Timber Point."

"Nice to meet you, Ted," said Millie feeling at ease. "What are you doing in town?"

"Paul invited us down to play some ball," replied Ted.

An exaggerated cough came from behind them.

Millie turned to see Paul standing at the worn-out spot that was home plate. He was wearing a catcher's mitt.

"Throw a few in here," he beckoned. Behind him was the old chicken wire backstop to keep the ball from going into the patch of forest, thick with thistles and pine trees.

Millie was startled by his friendliness.

"Um, sure," she said, lobbing the ball towards him.

A few throws in, and it was like old times. They silently tossed the ball back and forth. The pair kept up their pitch and catch routine for a while after Millie hit her growth spurt, but it quelled one day when they were playing at a Northside lot. Some older kids walking by told them that when they stood next to each other, they looked like the number 10. Millie, who was nearly a foot taller than Paul by then, tried to reassure him that they were just being jerks, but he never asked her to play catch again.

"I'm surprised you didn't come to the movie last night," said Paul

"Yeah, I haven't felt much like going out lately," responded Millie wistfully.

"Boy, you missed out," retorted Paul. "They even did a salute to soldiers, including George!"

"So, what are the rules?" asked Millie changing the subject.

"You throw the ball, we hit it," smirked Paul.

Millie threw one a little harder that popped his mitt.

"You been practicing?" asked Paul, surprised by her accuracy.

"I actually haven't picked up a ball since the meet," said Millie, equally as surprised.

Paul tried to zip it back to Millie, but the ball sailed over her outstretched glove.

"Must be a pretty bad throw if I can't reach it," quipped Millie.

One of the boys tracked it down, returning it to her.

"So, what are the ground rules?" She asked. Millie knew they always played the same game, but it was a ritual to ask. Besides, that's what the pros did.

"Pitcher's hand, ghost runners, and hitting it to right field is an out," he responded. Adding, "Unless you are left-handed, then hitting it to left field is an out unless you hit it over the shed."

"How about if the batter gets to call the field they want to hit to?" asked Millie, knowing it would irritate Paul.

"You asked me the ground rules, and I gave them to you," Paul barked back. He turned his back to the field and bent over to wipe an imaginary plate, shaking his rear end, which elicited laughs from the group. "Play ball," he yelled in his deepest voice.

The whole group laughed in unison. Millie thought Paul could be pretty funny when it wasn't directed at her.

Paul appointed himself team captain and leadoff batter. He acted like a big leaguer as he stepped into the box. The only thing he was missing was talent. To make matters worse, the home plate area was like quicksand. The more you dug in, the deeper you sank.

Paul had firsthand knowledge that Millie often had problems throwing strikes. With his bat resting on his shoulder, he watched Millie go into her herky-jerky windup. True to Millie's usual throws, the ball came in fast, but this one was right down the middle.

"Strike one," yelled Ted from shortstop.

"When I get one I can hit," bellowed Paul.

The next pitch was the same. Paul's bat remained on his shoulder.

"Strike two!" shouted Tim from the outfield.

"Hey," yelled Ted. "You plan on swinging?"

Paul tried to step out of the batter's box to yell back but tripped over his shoelaces, making him even madder. When he got to his feet, he muttered at Millie, "A fine time for you to learn how to pitch."

Paul was swinging before the third pitch was barely out of Millie's hand. He corkscrewed himself, tumbling to the ground. He picked up a handful of dirt and threw it. The boys in the field hid their smiles behind their gloves.

Millie continued to throw strikes. When Paul's team swung, they usually missed. She couldn't believe her accuracy from warm-ups carried over into the game. The ball went wherever she wanted, no matter how hard she threw. Paul and his teammates barely touched the ball. When they did, all they could muster were dribblers back to Millie.

After three innings of hitless ball, Millie's team led, 6-0.

"I'm gonna pull my team off the field if you don't swap out pitchers," Paul threatened.

Ted reluctantly took the mound, and Millie ran out to the outfield. "Nice throwing, lefty," he said as they passed each other, and she tossed the ball his way.

For a moment, she could breathe. She crouched down in centerfield, pulling out tufts of grass and soaking in the late morning sun.

Millie spotted Coach Shellman's beat-up car, painted in River Junction Central High red and white, parked down a side street. He tried to peer over a newspaper, watching the game inconspicuously, but no one in town had an old jalopy like his.

Millie had no idea how long coach had been sitting there. She knew he drove around looking for kids playing. His coaching and assessing of talent were never out of season. The only time he made his presence known was when he gave a quick honk of the horn when Millie crossed home plate, scoring a run. Shortly after Millie stopped pitching, he was gone.

When the game ended, Millie's team had won, 12-3.

"We'll have to play again," said Paul, who never took defeat easily.

"Yeah," Ted replied. "We should do a rematch when you come up to Timber Point for the fall jamboree."

"Sounds good," Paul said, already strategizing for the next time they met.

"You should bring Millie," added Ted genuinely, causing Paul to ride off on his bike in a huff.

CHAPTER 8

Following church on Sunday, Millie and her mother took the long way home, momentarily forgetting about their gasoline ration. Driving through town, they noticed recent events had reinvigorated River Junction's patriotism.

Not lacking in allegiant gestures, to begin with, residents seemed refreshed. New flags were out, and fresh patriotic bunting adorned eves and porches. The red, white, and blue were more vibrant than ever. They also noticed many people in their yards working on Victory Gardens. As the truck rolled past, they were greeted with waves.

Millie thought about the garden from the first spring that George was in the service. It was the last they planted as a family. At the end of the summer, Millie's father was killed, and her mother went to work at the Ordnance Plant.

"I know it's late in the season, Millie, but what do you say we get a Victory Garden going again?" said her mother breaking Millie's train of thought. "That could be our Sunday volunteer activity."

Millie's eyes lit up. "Sure," she replied without hesitation. She was starting to feel a bit neglected by all the time her mother spent with the Red Cross over at the Armory.

"Well, there is no better time to start than now," her mother said with excitement in her voice. "Why don't we head back to the house and get started?"

Millie and her mother breathlessly made plans.

"First, we need to weed all that grass," suggested Millie.

"Then we need to till," responded her mother. The soil had been neglected for nearly two years.

"Do you think we have time to grow something to enter into the fair?" asked Millie.

The conversation abruptly ended when they saw Coach Shellman emerge from behind the tannery shed.

It was mid-morning, and he was drenched in sweat. His customary khaki pants and white t-shirt were stained with dirt. He flashed his tobacco-stained half-smile—that looked more like a grimace—as he walked towards the truck, waving a newspaper.

"I called, but no one answered the phone, so I thought we'd come over," he said, jutting his thumb behind him. He turned and saw that he was alone. "Bah! Anyway, look at this here! Look at it!" he said in a gruff squeak of excitement, stuffing the newspaper in Millie's face before she could get out of the truck.

Millie was taken aback by coach's enthusiasm. Just then, Mr. Christopher appeared from around the corner of the shed. Sweat dripped from his brow. He had abandoned his customary tie. His sleeves were rolled up and his forearms were caked with dirt.

"What's this all about, Orville?" inquired Millie's mother in an unsure tone. She took the newspaper from coach's hand and placed herself between Millie and him.

"Millie, did you hear about the Reds' game yesterday?" asked coach excitedly over her mother's shoulder.

"Uh, um, no, coach," responded Millie apprehensively.

Millie's mother glanced at it, shrugged, and handed her daughter the periodical. Circled was the box score of a game between the Cincinnati Reds and St. Louis Cardinals that ended in an 18-0 Cardinals victory.

"So, what's so special about a game of baseball in Cincinnati that's got you digging around my yard on the Sabbath, Orville?" questioned Millie's mother in a teasing tone.

"I could see if it was a Cubs game or something," Millie added playfully, stepping behind her mother to hide her smile from the ribbing that coach was getting.

Coach didn't realize they were having fun at his expense. He poked his dirty finger at the newspaper, sweat smudging the newsprint. "See that player by the name of Nuxhall. That boy is all of 15 years old."

Both Millie and her mother's eyebrows raised in interest as they reviewed the box score.

"Now, his numbers aren't impressive, to say the least," added coach. "He didn't even make it through one inning, but I tell you, if the majors are gonna start taking boys barely in high school, then girls ain't gonna be far behind if the war continues," he said, nodding towards Millie.

The inference made Millie blush. She came out from behind her mother, standing in her shadow.

"I tell you what, Helen, that daughter of yours has a lightning bolt in her left arm," said coach, pointing at Millie. "I want her to be suiting up for my squad this summer. We only have a few games scheduled, but I know she could help us."

"Are you sure about this, Orville?" said Mrs. Bauer, surprised by his statement. "She's not even in high school."

"I'm positive, Helen," said coach wiping the perspiration off his forehead with the back of his hand. "I ain't never seen a girl throw a baseball like that. George was the last boy I seen that could sling a ball like Millie at this age."

"Aren't you getting a little ahead of yourself?" inquired Mrs. Bauer skeptically. "Saying she's going to pitch in the major leagues is a little outrageous when she hasn't even thrown a pitch in a high school game. Heck, she hasn't even thrown a pitch in a game other than on the sandlots."

Before Coach Shellman could respond, Mr. Christopher chimed in. "Even if she doesn't play high school ball…."

"Oh, she's gonna be playing," said Coach, cutting him off. "Mark my words! I'm losing more and more boys to this war and will need her if it continues."

"All right," said Mr. Christopher, pushing his spectacles up, only to have them slide back down his sweaty nose. "Even if she just plays high school ball, I can guarantee that she could play in the All-American Girls League."

"That's right," chimed in coach. "In fact, one of my old teammates manages the new Minneapolis outfit."

Millie first heard of the All-American Girls Professional Baseball League last year when an article appeared in the *Review* for a tryout at Wrigley Field in Chicago. There were teams all over the Midwest. The six-team league had recently added two teams—the Minneapolis Millerettes and Milwaukee Chicks—for its second season.

Mrs. Bauer seemed to be warming to the idea. "You still haven't answered my question, gentlemen."

"What's that, Helen?" Replied Coach Shellman.

"Why on earth are you two digging around my yard?" she said with a perplexed look.

"Come and take a look for yourself, ladies," said Coach Shellman, leading the pair behind the tannery shed.

Millie and her mother couldn't believe their eyes when they saw what the two men had done. On the back of the shed was a freshly painted catcher in Central High School red and white. Sixty-feet-and-six-inches away was a freshly manicured pitcher's mound, where just hours earlier sat a small hill of grass and weeds.

"There's one more thing, Millie," said Coach. "If it's okay with your mother, I'd like you to come over to Badger Park tomorrow and take part in some baseball drills. Most of last year's varsity will be there, along with a few of the hopefuls for this year's team."

Millie was taken aback. She was registered for Mount Popple, where she begrudgingly had been the last few years. She looked over at her mother for approval.

"I'll let Millie go to that playground on two conditions," said her mother, stone-faced.

"You name 'em," said coach enthusiastically.

"You need to promise me that she doesn't get hurt," she said, wiggling her index finger at Coach Shellman.

"You have my word on that," coach replied, putting his hand over his heart.

"And the second, Helen?" Chirped Mr. Christopher, who didn't realize he wasn't part of the conversation.

She looked over at the newspaper reporter and wiggled a finger at him and then back at coach. "Before you two leave this yard, you are going to help us with our Victory Garden."

"It's a deal," said a beaming coach. He extended his hand to Mrs. Bauer before realizing how dirty it was and pulling it back.

"So where does your garden grow?" said a giddy Mr. Christopher, happy to get a scoop for the newspaper.

CHAPTER

Millie was relieved as she climbed Pine Avenue hill towards Badger Park.

She stopped by the public library to check the *Review*. Once again, to her relief, George's name failed to appear in the military reports.

If there were nothing in the mail today, it would be 36 days since their last correspondence.

"No news is good news," she said aloud, reaching into the pocket of her overalls, feeling the telegram.

Millie began to fret about the park. Her mind swirled. *Who is going to be there? Do they even want me there? What is expected of me?*

Millie thought back to when she tagged along with George to Badger Park. Though it was just a few years ago, she couldn't remember much beyond going into the brush to get foul balls or slipping away to the bathhouse and then down the stairs to the Clearwater River. She spent what seemed like hours jumping off logs until George and his teammates would join for a dip before heading home.

On her way down the other side of Pine Avenue hill, Millie could see Badger Park in the distance. Her stomach fluttered. A handful of players had already congregated, loudly laughing and playing pepper. They noticed her approaching. A few of them looked her way before resuming the game.

Millie contemplated running home or up towards Mount Popple, where she could sit, do crafts, and maybe throw some horseshoes. She kept her head down. When she looked up, she was surprised to see they had stopped their game of pepper and turned in her direction. Her feet carried her right up to the group of high school boys.

"You want to play some pepper, Little Bauer?" asked Walter Edwards, standing in the foreground to greet her.

"I think I'll just watch for a while," Millie said, fidgeting with her new glove. She badly wanted to. She had loved watching George play prior to practice and games. Instead, she bashfully looked back down at the ground.

"You waiting for the newspaper reporter to get here?" chirped another boy, eliciting an outburst of laughter.

He jaunted over and playfully tapped the bill of her cap with his mitt. "I'm just kidding ya, Little Bauer. I'm Charlie Grogan. Glad you're here."

"They said they would be here a little after nine for my interview," she said with a toothy grin.

Millie's quick retort got an even bigger laugh from the group.

Charlie stepped back toward Millie and pulled her cap over her eyes, joining in on the laughter.

"Whoa, nice, Bauer," he said incredulously, grabbing the glove from her right hand. "That's a solid piece of leather!"

The other team members gathered around, admiring the mitt.

"Hey, Bauer, Coach Shellman wants everyone to sign in," said Walter pointing towards a clipboard on the ground.

"Can you come back and sign my glove when you are done?" asked Charlie, getting another light-hearted jab in, evoking a smattering of laughs. He was clearly the team clown.

Feeling more at ease, Millie walked towards the clipboard and signed in. When she turned back around to watch the game of pepper, Art Warren's green Dodge Brothers pickup was pulling up at the west end of the park. She was excited that he would be a part of the playground activities. Her heart sank, though, when Paul emerged from the cab and sauntered towards the group. Art honked his horn and pulled away with a wave.

Millie was certain that Paul wasn't going to be on the baseball team. Others thought the same.

"He must have inherited the equipment manager and scorekeeper position from his brother," said someone from the back of the group.

The arrival of Paul failed to generate the same fanfare that Millie had. The players seemed not to take notice. They resumed the game of pepper with Paul standing on the periphery.

"You better back up, Red, unless you want some free dental work," Charlie shouted to Paul.

Millie snorted with laughter. Paul shot an icy glare at her before returning his focus to the game.

"Why don't you go sign in on the clipboard, Warren," said Walter, gesturing towards Millie.

Millie instinctively moved a few steps away from the clipboard as Paul approached.

"Shouldn't you be up at Mount Popple weaving baskets or making paper lanterns?" Paul said smugly.

"I was going to ask you the same thing," countered Millie.

"Are you just here to watch or what?" responded Paul, raising his voice. "Because I'm the team manager now."

"Actually, Coach Shellman invited me to come here today," said Millie calmly.

Unbeknownst to Paul and Millie, the game of pepper had stopped, and the players were now listening to what was transpiring.

"You know the only reason you are here is because of who your brother is," shouted Paul.

"I guess I could say the same to you then, couldn't I, Pauley," said Millie in a calm tone. She knew he hated to be called that.

"I bet you'll be carrying equipment for me by the end of the season, Mildred," he said, his face matching the color of his hair.

Before Millie could respond, Coach Shellman marked his arrival with a whistle.

"Paul Warren," shouted Coach. "You march those hindquarters over here, and let's have a little talk."

Paul sheepishly turned around. "Yes, coach," he responded, slinking away from Millie.

'You trying to start a rhubarb with one of my players, son?" chastised coach.

"No, coach," responded Paul, shoulders slouched.

"I know you boys are already warmed up from playing pepper, but why don't you go ahead and take a few laps around the park? Give Bauer a tour of the grounds," instructed coach. He put a firm hand on Paul's shoulder and guided him over to a spot under a large elm tree.

Millie jogged over to the group and began running with them.

"Now, son, I ain't never cut a manager from a ball team," she heard coach say.

The team started talking amongst themselves, except for Walter Edwards, who ran a few strides ahead of the pack. Millie took up pace with Charlie in the rear. He was already breathing heavily.

"I'm sure Warren is getting an earful right now," he said with a wheezing laugh.

"I bet," she responded.

Millie actually felt sorry for Paul. She knew how much he loved River Junction Central High School sports, especially baseball. It would devastate him not to be a part of the team.

When the group made their way back around, coach yelled out, "Bauer come over here. Boys, take one more, clear out those lungs".

Millie maintained her jog over to Paul and Coach Shellman.

"Yes, coach?" she said, out of breath.

"Mr. Warren has something to say to you," replied Coach.

Millie looked over at Paul. His eyes were fixed on the ground, but she could see that his cheeks were stained with tears.

"Sorry for disrespecting you and your baseball abilities," Paul said, choking back tears and holding out a trembling hand. Coach had obviously told him what to say.

Millie paused and looked over at coach, who raised his eyebrows and gave an exaggerated nod towards Paul. The two former friends exchanged a quick handshake, avoiding eye contact. This is not what Millie was expecting on her first day of practice.

CHAPTER

Millie quickly fell into a routine over the next few days. She awoke early to eat breakfast with her mother and then tend to the Victory Garden. By eight o'clock, Millie was on the front steps of the public library, hand in her pocket, clutching the telegram, awaiting the doors to be unlocked. Often the first inside the library, Millie rushed to the newspaper reading room, grabbed that day's *Review,* and discreetly scanned it for any word of George's status.

On Friday, there was no mention of George, so Millie's burden was somewhat lessened for the day. She easily traversed the incline and decline of Popple Avenue hill on her way to Badger Park but was surprised to see none of the players on the field. Instead, they had congregated under the large elm tree where coach had chastised Paul. In the middle of the group was Coach Shellman. He greeted her as warmly as he knew how, "Take a seat there, Bauer. We are waiting on a few more people."

Millie sat quietly while others chatted. Coach Shellman came over and sat next to her. "That Warren boy not giving you any more guff, is he?" coach asked with a wink.

Millie smiled, looked down, and shook her head no.

Almost on cue, Art pulled up in his truck. Instead of merely dropping off Paul, he parked and exited the vehicle alongside his brother. The pair made the long walk across the park with all eyes on them. "Thanks for coming today, Warren," said coach, greeting Paul with a hearty handshake and a slap on the back. "We have a lot of work to do."

Coach turned his attention to the team. "There is not going to be any baseball today," he said sternly. He paced back and forth in front of the team like a general, head down, arms behind his back. "Now, before any of you start hemming and hawing, let me tell you what we are going to do."

Stopping in the middle of the group, he turned towards them. "We are going to do some good today," he said.

"Sick of those girl scouts showing us up, coach?" shouted Charlie Grogan from the back row, setting off a burst of laughter.

"Quiet in the peanut gallery, quiet in the peanut gallery," responded coach, shaking his head. He let the snickering die down before he continued.

"Every Friday, we are going to do our part in this war effort," he said. "Today, we are going to do a scrap paper drive."

There were no wise remarks from anyone when he revealed their plan.

"We are going to split up into two groups," he explained, holding up two fingers. "This half will go in Warren's truck and head across the river towards Riverbank Road," he said, dividing half the group down the middle with his hand. "This half will stay with me on this side of the river."

Millie looked around and saw that she had been put in coach's group. She was happy that she wouldn't have to deal with Paul but would have liked to have been able to talk to Art. She desperately wanted to show him her new glove.

"Any questions?" Coach asked. The group turned around, anticipating a wisecrack from Grogan. Even coach looked at him, but there was no response.

"All right, troops, dismissed," Coach shouted. The group jumped to their feet and headed for their respective vehicles.

Millie lagged behind, making the walk across the field alongside coach.

"You sit shotgun with me, Bauer," he insisted.

"Sure, coach," she said. Millie didn't have much of a choice as her group piled into the bed of the truck.

Before hopping in the cab, coach warned the players in the back. "No horseplay back there, or you'll be weeding Bauer's Victory Garden. If you think I'm tough, wait till Mrs. Bauer is giving you directives."

It was a short drive downtown; which coach spent much of pantomiming threats to Charlie Grogan, who was horsing around in the bed.

"That Grogan is a ham but a darn good backstop," said coach shaking his head and managing a chortle.

Coach parked the truck, and the players jumped out.

"Each of you grab a potato sack," coach ordered.

"I want you three to go south and you three to head north. Meet back here in an hour." The players grabbed their sacks and quickly dispersed.

Millie was in the group headed south, her sights on Delta Cinema. It had been ages since she stepped foot in the ornate building. She used to go with her parents and George at least once a month. Sometimes the siblings sat together on the balcony. Once in the lobby, she was overwhelmed by a waft of popcorn. Her mouth immediately began to salivate.

"First show doesn't start until noon," said a teenage boy behind the counter.

"Actually, I'm part of the River Junction Central High baseball team. I was wondering if there was any scrap paper that you wanted to donate," replied Millie. She was surprised at the way that sounded—*part of the River Junction Central High baseball team.*

The boy behind the counter seemed to be taken off guard as well. "Oh, um, let me go see," he replied, slipping from behind the desk into an office.

Millie became immersed in the sights and smells of the old theater's lobby, looking over the posters.

"Here you go," said the voice of a man behind her.

When Millie turned around, she saw the familiar face of Mr. Bronson, the owner of Delta Cinema. His youngest son had been one of the boys who had gone into the Army with George.

"Millie Bauer," he said enthusiastically, coming from behind the counter with a large box of scrap paper. "I didn't know you were on the team."

Millie nodded and smiled.

"Well, I did see that picture of you in the paper," he said, putting down the box and throwing an imaginary ball. He put his hand above his brow to watch it disappear into the distance.

"That was you," said the boy behind the counter, seemingly impressed.

Millie nodded, feeling her face reddening from embarrassment.

"Are you related to George Bauer?" asked the boy.

Millie nodded again.

"You know, I was actually going to call your mother. I just got a newsreel in today, and darn if I didn't see George on it," said Mr. Bronson, matter-of-factly.

The hair on the back of Millie's neck stood up. "Really," she said, trying to quell her excitement. "How can you tell?"

"He had that George Bauer swagger," said Mr. Bronson with a big grin.

Millie didn't want to get her hopes up too high.

"Why don't you and your mother come on down sometime, and I'll give you a private screening?" he offered. "Actually, now that I think of it, if you and your mother want to come down Sunday morning after church, we can watch it a few different times."

Millie wanted to jump at the chance but remained polite. "Are you sure, Mr. Bronson? I don't want you to go out of your way?"

"No problem at all," he said with a smile. "I have to work on some last-minute details before the matinees."

"I'll talk to my mother," Millie replied, unsure of what her mother would say.

Mr. Bronson dropped the smile from his face and made a point of looking away. "Oh, Millie, I forgot. I will be in before church."

Mr. Bronson didn't have to say anything else. In their excitement, they had both forgotten that tomorrow was Father's Day.

Millie remembered she had plans, too. She and her mother were to go to her father's grave and then to church.

Millie remained composed. "What time will you be in?"

"About eight-thirty, kiddo," Mr. Bronson replied, regaining his broad smile.

Millie turned and started to walk towards the doors to leave the building, planning to run the minute she was outside.

"Say, Millie," said Mr. Bronson with a laugh. "Don't you want the paper?"

"Yes," she responded sheepishly.

CHAPTER

Early Sunday morning, Millie excitedly bounded into the kitchen. The day prior, her mother agreed to go to Delta Cinema to see if she could spot George. Mrs. Bauer didn't hesitate at the opportunity. It was obvious that she, too, was desperate to hear of George's whereabouts and whether he was safe.

The pair planned to visit Mr. Bauer's grave at High Point Cemetery, then to the theater, and, finally, St. Martin's for mass. They were tentatively going to spend the rest of the day in the Victory Garden.

Millie came to an abrupt stop when she saw her mother sitting in the breakfast nook. While Millie was gussied up in her Sunday best, her mother looked like she was heading out to the garden.

"You better get ready; we have to leave soon," Millie urged, sliding onto the bench opposite her mother, hoping that she hadn't changed her mind.

Mrs. Bauer shifted in her seat, clutching a cup of coffee and looking ragged. "I'm not going to be able to go with you today, Millie," she said, appearing more tired than usual. There were dark circles around her eyes.

Millie didn't hide her disappointment, wailing, "Mother, why?"

"I'm sorry, dear," said Mrs. Bauer remorsefully. "I got a call late last night that a group of soldiers came in on a midnight train, so I went over to the Armory barracks. I've been up all night and plan to go back after breakfast."

Millie was shocked. She never heard the phone ring. "What about going to the cemetery?" continuing to press her mother for answers.

"Your father would want me to go look after these boys," said her mother, trying to put her hand on Millie's.

Millie pulled away. "But, what about Father's Day!" she said exasperated.

"I'm sorry, Millie. There are a few of the boys that need around-the-clock care," replied Mrs. Bauer sternly. "After mass, you can call over to the Armory to tell me if you saw George and then…."

Millie couldn't believe that her mother had had such a change of heart since yesterday. Now she was putting other soldiers ahead of the memory of her husband and missing son.

"Don't you care about daddy?" said Millie sharply, cutting off her mother. "Don't you care about George?"

As soon as the words came out of her mouth, she regretted it.

Millie's mother's eyes immediately met her daughters with a look of astonishment. "Mildred Bauer! What if your brother was one of those boys?"

"Mother, I'm sor…" said Millie, trying to apologize.

Her mother didn't let her finish.

"I'm not going to sit here and listen to this disrespect," she said, getting up from the table. "I'll be home in time for supper, and I expect that garden to be tended to."

The room went eerily silent. Millie reached into her pocket and squeezed the telegram. She didn't want to go to the cemetery alone, and she no longer felt compelled to go to the cinema or church. Impulsively, she decided to go to the train depot and wait for George to arrive. Maybe if she were down there, he would somehow get off one of the trains.

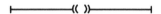

Millie sat on a bench at the railway platform, a train schedule in hand. This was the same platform that she and her mother ran the length of, crying alongside George's train, the day he left for basic training, the same platform that she saw her father wipe away the only tear she ever saw him shed during the same goodbye.

The 9:17 train arrived just as the schedule said. A woman dressed in a khaki military uniform stepped off the car onto the platform. With a calm, confident look on her face, she scanned the depot. Millie could tell this was her first time in River Junction when their eyes met. Millie smiled at the woman, who began walking directly at her.

"Hello, ma'am, my name is Lieutenant Baxter of the Women's Army Corps," she said, extending her hand, "WACS for short."

Millie looked over both her shoulders before realizing that the woman was talking to her. "Have you ever thought of joining the military?" inquired Lieutenant Baxter.

"Me?" said an incredulous Millie, shaking the woman's hand. People always thought she was older, especially when she was wearing her Sunday best.

"You are 20, aren't you?" inquired the woman.

"Why, yes, of course, I am," said Millie, forcing a laugh. She wasn't sure why she lied.

Millie knew all of the qualifications for a woman to become a member of the Women's Army Corps. She had seen the advertisements in newspapers and posters plastered all around town. Recruiters wanted to know if you were between the ages of 20 and 50, whether you had any children under the age of 14, and if you had at least two years of high school.

With their hands still interlocked, Millie stood up, hoping that her height would further support her fibbing. "In fact, I just turned 21," she added with confidence.

"Are you married?" inquired the Lieutenant.

"No, ma'am," replied Millie. "And I graduated from high school."

"Well, it sounds like you know where this conversation is heading," said the Lieutenant with a laugh. "Now, I'm just getting into town, and I don't have any of my information brochures here, but if you stop by the recruiting office tomorrow, we could maybe talk about your interests."

"What are your hours down there because I'm working at the ordinance plant?" replied Millie. She was surprised at how easily it came out of her mouth.

"A Rosie the Riveter," said the officer. "I should have known!"

Millie quickly flexed a Rose the Riveter pose which made the recruiter laugh.

"So, Rosie isn't your name," asked the officer, "or is it?"

Millie's mind went blank. "No, um, Millie…..Millie Warren,"

She wasn't sure why she said Warren.

"Nice to meet you, Ms. Warren," replied the officer. Her eyes suddenly went behind Millie, acknowledging someone's presence with a nod. Millie froze for a moment, hoping it wasn't someone she knew.

Millie turned to see another woman wearing the same uniform. She didn't know her but had seen her numerous times around town in the WACS Recruiting car. They had even exchanged pleasantries a few times when Millie passed by the recruiting station next to the Confluence Bank.

"Hello, Lieutenant Kent," said Lieutenant Baxter with a warm smile. "I was just talking to Millie Warren."

"Nice to meet you, Ms. Warren," said the woman, firmly shaking Millie's hand with a look like she had no recollection of the pair ever meeting.

"Millie is going to stop by the office to talk about some opportunities," said Lieutenant Baxter enthusiastically.

"Well, that's great," said Lieutenant Kent flashing the same warm, confident smile as Lieutenant Baxter. "You know there are nearly a dozen women from River Junction in uniform to date?"

"Really?" Millie replied, genuinely impressed.

"Do you live around here, Millie?" inquired Lieutenant Kent.

"Yes, I live in Shantytown and work over at the Ordinance Plant," the lies continued to roll off Millie's tongue.

"Is that so," said Lieutenant Kent, showing keen interest. "I thought I had talked to all the ladies over at the plant."

"What building do you work in?" she inquired. For a moment, Millie thought she looked like she was beginning to recognize her.

"Building number three," she said. She had heard her mother repeat this phrase numerous times.

"Munitions, right?" Said Lieutenant Kent with a befuddled look. "I must have missed you that day."

"You must have," said Millie starting to feel uncomfortable about her lies.

"Are you waiting for someone?" asked Lieutenant Baxter.

"Sort of," replied Millie, fidgeting. "His name is George."

"Was he supposed to be on this train?" Lieutenant Kent inquired.

Millie felt that if she stayed around any longer, she might blurt out that the whole conversation had been a lie.

"I thought so," said Millie. "Well, I guess I must have gotten my days wrong."

"Well, it was nice meeting you, Miss Warren," said Lieutenant Kent, abruptly ending the interaction, much to Millie's relief. She again firmly shook Millie's hand. "Lieutenant Baxter and I have an appointment we need to get to."

"I hope to see you soon down at the office," Lieutenant Baxter said, thrusting her hand into Millie's. "If not, I'll be stopping down at the factory."

Millie nodded and smiled. She had never had so many handshakes in that short a time. She breathed a sigh of relief, watching the women walk towards the WACS recruiting car. In the distance, she heard a church bell ring, signifying half past the hour. She quickly made her way off the platform towards St. Martin's.

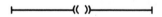

Millie's attention was lacking during the service, except when George's name was mentioned during a prayer of dedication for local service members. A few people turned in their pews and nodded at her. Otherwise, her mind raced.

When Millie returned home, she went inside to change her clothes to begin tending to the Victory Garden. She nearly yelped when she found her mother sitting at the dining room table.

"Hello, Millie," said her mother with a weary smile. She was in a much different mood than when they had parted ways that morning.

"Mother," said a visibly shaken Millie. "I thought you were spending the day over at the Armory with the group of soldiers that had just come in."

"I went over to the barracks and told them that I would be there later this afternoon and stay through the night," explained Mrs. Bauer.

"But I didn't see you at church," said a puzzled Millie. She couldn't remember the last time they didn't attend mass together.

"Well, I went over to the cinema where I thought you would be," said Mrs. Bauer with a raised eyebrow. "Mr. Bronson showed me the film, but I didn't see anyone that looked like George."

Millie's heart sank when she heard those words.

"I stopped over at *River Junction Book and Stationery* to buy this," said Mrs. Bauer, pointing at a shiny white scrapbook in front of her on the table. Millie hadn't noticed it. It was dwarfed by George's bulging book of accolades sitting beside it.

"What's that, Mother?" inquired Millie.

"I thought that since the *Review* is taking a liking to you, we should start a scrapbook of your own," replied Mrs. Bauer cheerily. She opened the cover. The picture and article from Millie's accomplishments at the Field Meet were matted on the first page.

A gush of pride washed over Millie. She leaned in, giving her mother an extended, warm embrace.

"I also restarted our subscription," her mother cheerfully added. "You won't have to rush out the door and over to the library before practice now."

Millie was tempted to tell her mother about the telegram burning a hole in her pocket.

"How about we head out and pull some weeds?" suggested Mrs. Bauer, tussling Millie's hair. "Go upstairs and throw on some weeding clothes."

CHAPTER

The more Millie practiced with the team, the more comfortable she became. By the end of the second week, she was taking part in the fast-paced pepper games prior to practice. Surprised how at ease she was around her teammates, Millie felt closer to George when she was around them, and, in some odd way, it made her feel that he might be safe.

Not all of the players were happy that she was there, though. She could feel the icy glares coming from soon-to-be-senior Johnny Green. He was big and broad-shouldered, and his biceps bulged out of the snug, heavy cotton baseball uniform. His one shortcoming was that he couldn't play baseball worth a lick. His real love was playing the trumpet, but his father, James Green, made him play baseball.

The Greens were one of the wealthiest families in town. They made their fortune during the lumber era when River Junction was the hub of the local timber trade. Mr. Green owned the paper mill and was a partial owner of the ordinance plant, where Millie's mother worked. For years he helped finance the sports teams at Central High School, taking a particular interest in baseball.

Each spring, the team had boxes of new balls, several new bats, and two sets of uniforms: a white one for playing at home and a grey for playing away from River Junction. Mr. Green also set up a deal with Buckley's Sporting Goods so ballplayers could get their equipment at a discounted rate. He would pay the difference.

There were strings attached. Mr. Green's financial involvement forced Coach Shellman to keep Johnny on the roster. Coach had been able to not play him under the guise of better upperclassmen in front of him, but now that Johnny was going to be a senior, coach was running out of excuses.

Over the last three years, Coach Shellman worked countless hours with Johnny, and when the Rafters were still playing in town, he got pitching lessons from their manager Rosy Ryan, who pitched ten years in the big leagues. Last fall, Johnny even got a pitching lesson from Burleigh Grimes, the great spitball pitcher, who was passing through town on his way to his cabin on Yellow Lake.

Millie noticed Johnny's disdain for her when she began improving each day. She always had a strong arm, but under the tutelage of Coach Shellman, she realized there was more to the game than just throwing it by a batter. Coach showed her a few different ways to grip a fastball. With her long, slender fingers, unique windup, and quirky delivery, the ball danced even more than usual.

"Hey, coach, you aren't teaching her to throw spitters, are you?" shouted an exasperated Charlie Grogan after he dropped to his knees and blocked another ball that dove into the dirt at the last second.

"I don't need to, Grog," piped back Coach Shellman. "That's all-natural movement!"

One grip, in particular, made the ball dart and dive, depending on where she put her index finger.

"We're gonna call that the 'dark one,'" coach told her giddily.

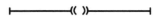

Millie awoke to disappointment on Friday. Rain pounded on the roof above her, but she held out hope that it would let up. She was looking forward to seeing the guys on the team—even Paul. She carried on with her normal morning routine, heading out to make sure the team wasn't doing their Friday volunteering.

Millie went as far as the library, figuring she might as well go to the park. But, walking down Popple Avenue hill, the weather worsened. A heavy, driving rain blew into her face, rendering her umbrella useless.

In the distance, she saw no one at the park. She turned to run home when a voice came through the downpour, "Hop in, Millie!"

Millie turned around to see Art Warren's truck. A brown tarp covering the truck bed whipped up, exposing a load of produce. Millie ran around to the passenger side, collapsed her umbrella, and hopped in.

"What the heck are you doing walking around in this monsoon, Millie?" asked Art, incredulously.

"I wasn't sure if the team was going to do any volunteering this week," replied Millie, her teeth chattering.

Art just shook his head, "You're as dedicated as your brother."

"What are you doing, Art?" asked Millie, water dripping from the bill of her drenched River Junction cap.

"I had to go pick up some produce out past McAlpine," he said. "You feel like helping me unload it?"

"Sure," said Millie. She hadn't been down to Warren's Grocery & Dry Goods since school dismissed for the summer.

The two chatted mainly about baseball and the weather. Before Millie knew it, they were driving down the alley along the river. Art backed the truck up to the backdoor and honked his horn twice.

"Paul and Don are supposed to be out here to help unload," said Art turning off the truck engine. "Let's just wait to see if they come out."

Within seconds, Art was tapping the wheel, visibly agitated. He honked the horn again, keeping his hand on it for a few extra seconds.

"Why don't we get out and start unloading?" said Millie, opening the door and letting in some rain. Art reached across Millie and shut the door.

"No," he said forcefully. "I'm sorry, Millie, but I want to see if this little weasel is going to get out and help."

Art honked the horn again. His cheeks were getting rosy. Something seemed to be bothering him.

After a few more minutes, Art recanted. "Fine, but I'm gonna go find him," he said gruffly as he slapped the wheel, stormed out of the truck, and disappeared into the store's back door.

Millie hopped out, grabbed a basket, and headed for the store's rear entry.

"Millie Bauer," said Mrs. Warren, coming out the back door just as Millie was about to balance the load on her knee to open it. "So nice to see you."

Mrs. Warren smiled warmly, holding the door ajar for Millie to get through.

"Hello, Mrs. Warren," replied Millie. She was glad to see Mrs. Warren, who always seemed to take a special interest in her. Maybe it was because she had three sons and no daughters.

"Millie Bauer, I swear you get taller every time I see you," gushed Mrs. Warren.

A snort came from behind Mrs. Warren as Paul came into the back room with his younger brother, Don. They had on their Boy Scouts uniforms.

"I bet she can chew gum and walk at the same time, too," said Paul sarcastically.

"Paul!" chastised Mrs. Warren, shooting a steely glare at her middle child. "You are already on your brother's bad side."

"Hi, Millie!" Paul said with fake enthusiasm.

"Hurry up, boys. Start getting this unloaded," ordered Mrs. Warren. "You two need to be at the bus depot by noon."

"I hear you and your mother started a Victory Garden," said Mrs. Warren, turning her attention back to Millie.

"Yes, Mrs. Warren," answered Millie shyly.

"Well, people still ask us about that Bauer Jam, so keep that in mind when you are canning this fall," said Mrs. Warren.

"Yes, ma'am," said Millie.

"Before I forget, I have an extra copy of the *Review* with your picture in it. What a dandy!" exclaimed Mrs. Warren.

"Thank you," replied a flattered Millie. She felt a sudden urge to hug Mr. Warren.

"There is something I want to talk to you about though, Millie," said Mrs. Warren looking concerned.

Just then, Art came from the front of the store. "Mrs. Krenell wants to see you, Ma," he said in a businesslike voice that had replaced the angry tone from earlier.

"All right, Art," she said before turning her attention back to Millie. "Make sure you talk to me before you leave," directed Mrs. Warren.

Millie wondered if perhaps she knew something about George.

"You can put them in the back storeroom, Millie," suggested Art, pointing to the bushel at her feet.

"Oh, okay," she said, grabbing the basket and heading into the store.

"Thanks," Art said as Millie passed. He seemed to have momentarily settled down.

Millie made her way toward the storage room. When she reemerged, Art, Paul, and Don were in the store talking. Art's cheeks were once again flushed.

"I hope the war is still going on when I'm old enough," said Paul puffing out his chest.

"Me, too," said Don, not really knowing what he was agreeing to.

"I heard Dad and Art talking about something that President Roosevelt just did that gives you all kinds of free stuff when you get done serving in the military," said Paul.

"Really," said Don, his eyes widening.

"Yeah, they even give you money for not working," continued Paul, looking over at Millie.

"It's called the Servicemen's Readjustment Act, and neither of you should want the war to be going on five years from now," said Art, visibly agitated.

"Just because you can't go doesn't mean that I can't," said Paul, obviously trying to hurt Art's feelings.

"I'd go in if I could," said Art, the red in his cheeks spreading to his ears and down his neck.

"What could you do besides push a pen?" Paul smugly retorted.

Millie had heard enough. She rushed over, towering behind Paul. "I think there are height requirements in the military."

Paul spun around with fire in his eyes. "If you keep growing, they'll have to put you in the circus," he retorted angrily.

Mrs. Warren entered the store carrying a bushel of tomatoes, unaware of the tense mood. "The rest of that stuff isn't going to walk its way in here, but if it sits out there unattended, it might just grow legs."

Millie and Paul glared at one another.

Mrs. Warren hadn't heard the argument. "Paul and Don, keep unloading that truck," she said, gesturing towards the back door. "Art, could you watch the store while Millie helps me in the back?"

Millie was still shaking. She and Paul exchanged another dirty look before the boys exited the back.

"Millie, can you please follow me?" requested Mrs. Warren.

Millie composed herself and followed close behind. "Yes, Ma'am"

Mrs. Warren sat down on the couch, patting the cushion next to her.

Millie obliged, nervously sitting down.

"A recruiter for the Women's Army Corps came into the store a few days ago looking for a Millie Warren," said Mrs. Warren

"Really?" said Millie sounding surprised. She hadn't given much thought to the consequences of her actions of the previous weekend.

"Yes, dear, and when she described the woman, she sounded an awful lot like you," continued Mrs. Warren.

"Hmmm," said Millie looking at the floor.

"She also said that she had been over at building three in the Ordinance Factory looking for, but there was no record of a Millie Warren," said Mrs. Warren.

Millie continued avoiding eye contact.

"Millie, what is this all about?" asked Mrs. Warren, sounding concerned.

Just then, Paul came busting through the door. "If you're done holding down the couch, Bauer, could you give us a hand with the rest of this?" He had sweat dripping off his reddened forehead.

Millie had never been so happy to see him.

"Paul Michael Warren!" said his mother opening her eyes widely and tilting her head. Her glasses slid to the end of her nose. "I'm sure your troop could find a way to survive without you."

"Yes, mother," said Paul sheepishly. "Sorry, Millie."

Mrs. Warren shooed Paul out of the back room before turning her attention back to Millie. "Why don't you go out and help the boys finish unloading the rest of the truck," she suggested with a softer tone than her son. "They could use some direction."

"Yes, Ma'am," said Millie with a little laugh.

"But, I hope I don't hear anything else of this," said Mrs. Warren, raising her eyebrows and pointing a finger at Millie.

"Yes, Ma'am," replied Millie sheepishly.

As the two rose from the couch, Millie awkwardly threw her arms around Mrs. Warren.

CHAPTER

Millie sat in the breakfast nook, eating oatmeal and reading the Saturday edition of the *Review*. The radio played inaudibly in the dining room. She enjoyed being able to comfortably read the paper at home rather than bustling over to the library. She didn't miss the queasy feeling of uncertainty climbing the cement steps. Alas, there was no word from George. It had now been 50 days since his last letter and 23 days since the glove and telegram were delivered minutes apart.

Millie moved on to the sports section to look at the box scores from Friday night's games. A headline on the side of the page caught her attention: *Millie Bauer to Pitch for Central High July 4 Game.*

The article read:

Millie Bauer, kid sister of former River Junction Central High School standout and current Army patriot, Private First Class George Bauer, is slated to pitch when they take on the River Junction County All-Stars on July 4.

The junior Bauer first caught the eye of Coach Shellman when she won the baseball toss at the annual City Meet for eighth graders. When asked how he decided on the young Bauer, Coach Shellman said, "I like what I've been seeing out of her during the playground season, so I figured we should take a look at what she can do."

Tickets for the game will be 50 cents for adults and 25 cents for children under 12. All proceeds will go to the War Effort.

Millie badly wanted to cut the article out and put it into her scrapbook but decided to wait until her mother got home to surprise her. She went looking for George's large red scrapbook to occupy her time and think of him in a positive way. She searched his room and atop the buffet in the dining room. Now that Millie was thinking about it, she hadn't really seen it since the Sunday that her mother had bought her one of her own.

Millie kept herself distracted throughout the day. After breakfast, she worked in the garden. Before lunch, she threw a bunch of pitches to the tannery shed catcher. Early in the afternoon, she took her ration stamps and coins to the grocery store and bought her allotted amount of sugar, butter, and milk for the upcoming week. Upon returning home, she scoured the house looking for George's scrapbook but, alas, found nothing.

Finally, Millie went to the Ordinance Plant to wait for her mother to finish. The quarter-to-five whistle sounded. She pedaled her bike towards the factory along the river. Women began pouring out of the buildings, heading home for the evening. Making her way to Building Three, Millie was met with smiles and hellos, but she didn't see her mother.

Millie saw a man whom she thought was the foreman of her mother's building. "Excuse me, sir, have you seen Helen Bauer?"

He gave her a confused look. "She wasn't in today. Said she had some urgent business to take care of."

Millie's mother hadn't been coming home after work all week, but Millie thought it was because she was just heading directly to Armory.

"Thank you, sir," said a baffled Millie.

In the distance, church bells rang for the six o'clock evening mass at St. Martin's. A few blocks from the church was Coach Shellman's house. Millie hopped on her bike and rode towards the bells.

Millie's mind raced as she made her way towards Coach's house. Before she knew it, Millie was looking up the sidewalk to the front steps of his house. She noticed the door was open. Instead of knocking, she cupped her hands on the side of her eyes and peered through the screen door.

"Coach?" she called meekly.

There was no answer, but she could hear humming coming from atop the stairs.

"Coach," she said more forcefully.

The humming stopped.

"Who is it?" said Coach Shellman.

"Millie Bauer," answered Millie.

"Bauer?" coach in a surprised tone. "Come on in, kid, I'll be right down."

Millie cautiously opened the screen door and entered the vestibule. She stood in the entry hallway, unsure how much farther she should go. To the right was a room that, in most houses, was a dining room. By the looks of it, coach had turned it into a sports storage facility. Hurdles, deflated basketballs, and football jerseys were strewn all over the floor.

"You comin' in, Bauer, or are you going to keep guard down there?" said coach. "Why don't you head into the living room and take a seat? I'll be right down."

Millie followed his orders and went to the room to the left. It was somewhat of a normal living room, except for the chalkboard in front of the fireplace. The room was lined with numerous photographs; many were of teams that he had coached over the years. A picture of coach and George held a prominent place on the wall. Millie reached in her pocket and squeezed the telegram.

A lone, faded snapshot sitting on an end table caught Millie's eye. She was stunned when she picked it up, a young, grinning Coach Shellman with someone who looked exactly like him. They were adorned in baseball uniforms with arms draped around each other's shoulders.

"Me and my brother, Dave," said coach, startling Millie.

Millie turned to see coach dressed in something besides khaki pants and a grey sweatshirt. He had on a navy blue suit and tie.

"Hi, Coach," said Millie. "I didn't know you had a brother."

"Yep, twins," he replied. "That picture was taken in June 1917, the last game we played together. The next day we enlisted in the Army."

"Where does he live?" she asked.

"Well, Bauer, he only lives in pictures and dreams now," said Coach. "He was killed in World War I."

Millie was aware that Coach had served in World War I but had no idea that his twin brother was killed in the fighting. She ached to tell coach about George, but all she did was reach in her pocket and squeeze the telegram again.

"So, you played baseball together?" asked Millie, trying to change the subject.

"We sure did. One of the best double play combinations in the Cutover County Farm League," said coach with a wink.

Millie knew better. She remembered her father saying Coach would have made it to the pros had he not broken his ankle sliding into second base when he was playing minor league ball in Nashville.

Coach changed the subject altogether. "I take it you saw the paper?" He asked.

"I did," she said with a smile. "Are you sure?"

"I wouldn't have done it if I didn't have complete faith in you, Bauer," said coach.

"What about Johnny Green?" asked Millie.

"He'll get some tosses," said coach.

"What about Mr. Green?" rebuked Millie.

"Heck, he can toss a few if he wants," said coach. "Is there anything else you want to discuss, Bauer, or were you trying to ask your way out of the lineup?"

Millie paused and thought about why she had come to his house. "No, coach," she said.

"Well, if that's all, I need to make my way down to the Legion Hall for a Bond Drive Ball. Gonna dance our boys to victory," said coach. He grabbed a straw boater hat off the coat rack and planted it atop his head. The navy blue ribbon around matched his suit and tie.

"You want me to throw that bike in the back of my truck and give you a ride, Bauer?" coach asked.

"No thanks, coach," responded Millie. She had a lot on her mind, and the ride home gave her time to think.

CHAPTER

There was no mention of George in the *Review*. No letter from him, either. Millie never confronted her mother about not being at work. After all, Millie wasn't being completely honest, too. Besides, they barely saw each other. Each morning her mother said she was on the way to the factory. If she did come home at night, she arrived after Millie was in bed. She was lucky if her mother stopped in to say goodnight or ask how her day was.

On Monday, July 3, the baseball team had a special practice at Lumbermen Park, where the uniforms were to be distributed by Mr. Green. Millie had never witnessed the disbursement, but she remembered George making fun of the way Mr. Green called up each player and made a big presentation. A photographer accompanied him to take a picture of each of them receiving the jersey. Mr. Green made sure the picture of him and George made the front page of the *Review*.

Millie was shocked when she arrived at the park. A large crowd in the grandstands awaited the practice.

"There hasn't been a crowd like this since your brother was playing," said Charlie Grogan, while they jogged around the field.

Among the onlookers was Mr. Green, following Coach Shellman around. He chomped on an unlit cigar, dispensing unsolicited advice whenever possible. Coach just nodded, his jaw pulsating with annoyance.

Mr. Green hovered around the pitchers while they worked out, now smoking the cigar. When it was Johnny's turn, he shouted at his son in between every toss. Of the younger Green's thirty pitches, only a handful were strikes.

When Millie took the mound, a crowd congregated behind the home plate screen and along the edge of the field. 'Ooh's' and 'aah's' arose from the group as she displayed near-perfect control. She glanced over at Mr. Green, who was silent. He repeatedly stroked his pencil-thin mustache, his face growing redder with each strike she threw.

After her pitching session, Mr. Green approached her. "Nice throwing, Ms. Bauer," he said with no sincerity in his voice.

"Thank you, Mr. Green," replied Millie.

"I thought you were only on the team because of who your brother was," he said, emphasizing the word 'was.' "I see you can actually pitch."

He threw his cigar on the ground and put it out with his heel before walking away.

Millie stood frozen. She was stuck on the way he said, 'was.'

The interaction left Millie in a daze for the rest of practice. Her state of mind didn't get any better when it came time to hand out uniforms.

It seemed that all of the players knew what to expect when their names were called. They each approached Mr. Green, thanked him loud enough for everyone to hear, and then posed for a picture. After Charlie Grogan received his jersey, he bowed to the crowd still looking on. Coach half-heartedly yelled, "Grogan," while Mr. Green glared at the catcher.

The last two people without a uniform in their possession were Millie and Paul. After Paul's name was called, it was apparent there were no jerseys left.

Mr. Green knew exactly what he was doing.

"Oh, Ms. Bauer, it seems that we are all out of uniforms," he said with a devious grin. "I thought you were simply going to be some sort of mascot, a tribute to your brother, per se."

Millie could feel her ears getting red. Again, he was speaking of George in the past tense.

"I thought we spoke about this, Green," coach said angrily.

"Sorry, coach," Mr. Green said condescendingly. "If I had known how good she was, I would have made sure she got one."

Millie was afraid she would burst into tears if she looked up.

"She can have mine," said a voice behind her.

"Now, Mr. Edwards, that's very noble of you, but….," started Mr. Green.

Walter Edwards was holding out his new jersey, offering it to Millie.

"I'll handle this matter, Edwards," said coach cutting him off. "Don't you have someone else to talk down to, Green?"

"I don't think that I like your tone, Mr. Shellman," replied a blustery Mr. Green.

"I don't think I like you," snapped coach. "I'm tired of this pomp and circumstance."

"We'll talk about this another time then," said Mr. Green storming off through the crowd of onlookers.

"You can guarantee it," yelled coach after Mr. Green. "Your deep pockets don't intimidate me."

Coach didn't wait for the crowd to disperse before addressing the team.

"If any of you have a problem with Millie Bauer being on this team, I want you to get up and leave right now," he growled, looking around at the players seated on the grass.

"Some of you are lucky even to have a roster spot," he said, directing his comment toward Johnny Green.

"As far as a uniform goes," he said, addressing the matter at hand. "I appreciate the offer, Edwards, but we don't need any chivalry."

"Sir Edwards of River Junction," snipped Charlie, jabbing Walter in the ribs.

"I didn't hear you offering up yours, Grogan," retorted coach. "Edwards did what captains are supposed to do."

"I don't think she could fit into mine," quipped Grogan.

"True," was all coach could say.

Laughter eased the tense situation.

"There are plenty of old jerseys around. We'll figure something out," said coach. "Now go enjoy the rest of the day. Remember, you may never play in front of a bigger crowd than tomorrow, so be ready."

While the rest of the team left, coach pulled Millie aside and dispensed some advice. "Don't worry about Green. He isn't too happy that you have more baseball talent in your pinkie than his son."

Suddenly, Millie had an idea. "What do you think about me wearing one of George's old uniforms?" She said.

Coach smiled slowly, "I think that's a great idea, Millie—and a fitting tribute."

"I'm pretty sure they are still in his closet," said Millie enthusiastically.

"Make 'em wonder if it's you or George out there," said coach with a laugh.

CHAPTER  15

Millie and her mother ate breakfast and then tended to the Victory Garden. Their hard work was already paying dividends, with multiple crops sprouting up. There was even some talk of entering something in the Western Wisconsin District Fair.

"It's too late to do any preserves," said her mother, "but maybe we can do a pie."

If anything was burdening either of them, they didn't let on.

Millie was excited that her mother was going to see her pitch. The factory was closed on account of the holiday, and her mother was going to bring some of the wounded soldiers from the barracks over to the game.

In the afternoon, Millie and her mother went up to George's room to retrieve one of his uniforms. Millie had tried them on numerous times over the years but never wore one outside the confines of the house. When they opened the closet, Millie was surprised to see only two as opposed to the usual three.

"I think you should wear this one," said her mother, pulling out the cream-colored jersey from George's sophomore year and holding it up to Millie. As they were leaving the room, Millie also noticed George's favorite picture of Bob Feller missing from above his bed.

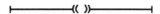

Millie put on George's heavy wool uniform, tucked the telegram in her back pocket, and walked over to meet her teammates. Together, they headed over to Popple Avenue to be part of the Fourth of July parade to Lumbermen Park. Millie was still feeling nervous about how she looked in the baggy uniform,

Walter Edwards came over. "It looks great, kid" he said reassuringly.

Around six o'clock, Millie and her teammates lined up with their opponents, the River Junction County All-Stars. The All-Stars were mostly men who weren't accepted into the military for various reasons. Several weren't serving because they received farm deferments. It was easy to imagine that George could have been granted one if the Bauer's farm was still active.

The streets were lined with cheering people—young and old. The team marched down Parbuckle Avenue, turned on Riverbank Road, and headed towards the ballpark. In front of the ball players were soldiers in training from the Armory, marching in unison. Again, Millie couldn't help but think of George. Not that her thoughts were ever far from him.

When the group arrived at the stadium, they had a short warm-up session as the crowd took their seats. The two teams then retreated to their respective dugouts, and the coaches met at home plate to exchange lineups, discuss the park's ground rules, and flip a coin to decide who would be the home team.

The magnitude of the game didn't hit Millie until she was standing in the dugout waiting to take the mound. The grandstands were packed, and there was a whole section of the soldiers who participated in the parade. Millie didn't even entertain the idea of scanning the group for George, but she did see her mother right away. She was sitting in the front row next to the injured soldiers. There was one whose head was heavily bandaged, covering his face, another with his arm in his sling, and yet others appeared to be perfectly fine.

It was nearing dusk, but the sun was still extremely hot. Wearing the heavy wool uniform, Millie had already begun to sweat profusely. Her back was drenched, and beads of sweat rolled from her forehead. She felt nauseous but was momentarily calmed by an unlikely person.

"Do you remember that time you got in trouble for stealing that baseball?" asked Paul, appearing by Millie's side.

Millie nodded. "You mean when *you* stole the ball," she said with a relieved smile.

Millie and Paul were eight years old and had walked over to Lumbermen Park to watch a ballgame by themselves. They didn't have any money, so they stood outside, waiting for a foul ball to leave the park.

Baseballs were expensive, so the team had people tracking down the ones that left the stadium. If you gave it back to them, you were allowed into a game for free. Sometimes kids still tried to steal them, though.

The pair had barely arrived at the park when they heard a crack of a bat. Suddenly, a ball came zipping past before they could react. They looked at each other and went after it. Paul reached it first, picked it up, and kept on running as fast as his legs could carry him. He didn't make it far before a Lumbermen Park employee sped by Millie, who stood frozen. The man caught up to Paul and easily wrestled the ball away from him.

When the employee was walking back to the stadium past Millie, he recognized her. "Hey, aren't you Jim Bauer's kid?" he angrily asked. Millie didn't answer, but she didn't need to. "He'll hear about this," he said before running back to the ball field. Millie was grounded for two weeks.

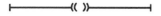

"All right," said Coach Shellman, halting the interaction between Paul and Millie. "We're home team. Go get 'em, Bauer," he said, tossing a ball to Millie.

The teams formed a "V" for victory formation on either side of the pitcher's mound for the national anthem. Johnny Green walked out into the middle of the infield with his trumpet and played a stirring version of "Taps," which led into the national anthem.

The beauty of his playing and the silence of the crowd made Millie shudder. Her nerves were unbearable during warm-ups tosses. The few didn't even make it to home plate, bounding up and over Grogan. He jogged a new ball out to her, but that did nothing to calm her down.

Nausea washed over Millie when the first River Junction County All-Star came walking to the plate. It was Scott Nelson, who had played with George in high school. He was a small left-handed hitter, nicknamed "Scooter" because he could run like a deer.

Before Scooter stepped into the batter's box, he gave a subtle tip of the cap to Millie. His hospitality ended there, though, when he ripped the first pitch he saw directly at the right fielder.

One of the great parts about Lumbermen Park was that the dimensions and layout were exactly like Wrigley Field, where the Chicago Cubs played. However, this was unfortunate for whoever was playing right field, because by mid-afternoon, they were looking directly into the sun. Poor Stan Johnson. He never moved when Scooter's ball rocketed right by him, coming within inches of hitting him in the head. By the time Stan tracked the ball down at the fence, Scooter was already rounding third base and heading for home. Stan's throw sailed over the cutoff man's head and rolled to a stop a few feet from Millie.

When Millie turned around, Grogan was at the mound to calm her. "Well, we got that one taken care of," he said into his mitt. "What do you say we get the next three out?"

This isn't facing Paul Warren at the sandlot, Millie thought, stepping back on the pitcher's rubber. She looked over at Coach Shellman, standing on the top step of the dugout. He gave a whistle, nodded, and clapped his hands. He didn't say anything, but seeing his confidence calmed Millie.

The next batter was an older man that Millie didn't recognize. From the chatter in the County All-Stars dugout, his name was "Vern."

Millie went into her unusual windup and delivery, throwing a strike right down the middle. The man nodded in agreement at the call and did the same when the next pitch went by. Grogan signaled for the "dark one." Millie went into her windup and slung a perfect toss. The pitch looked like it was going to hit Vern square in the ribs. He lunged to avoid the ball and didn't see it cross over the inside corner of the plate for strike three. This time he merely shook his head in disbelief.

As he walked back to the dugout, he turned back to the umpire and said, "Better check that ball. She's putting something on it, blue."

This brought coach out of the dugout. "It doesn't matter if she is, Vern," he shouted. "You have to take the bat off your shoulder to hit."

The third batter decided to take the same approach as Scooter, attacking the first pitch. Millie threw another "dark one." The ball appeared to be right down the middle. At the last second, it dropped down and away from the batter, who swung feebly, not even close to hitting the ball. The pitch sent Grogan sprawling to catch it. The ball rolled all the way to the backstop. The batter, anticipating the same thing, watched the following two pitches, both strikes. He, too, was left shaking his head as he retreated to the dugout.

Millie started the next batter off with her specialty pitch, but it didn't move. Instead, it was a fastball right down the middle. The batter hit it square toward Walter Edwards at shortstop, who didn't have to move.

"Good inning, Bauer," he said, gliding past her on the way back to the dugout.

It was much of the same the next two innings, with Millie keeping the All-Stars off balance with her mix of pitches. The only other hit she gave up was an infield single to Scooter Nelson with two out in the top of the third.

As Millie jogged back to the dugout after striking out Vern for a second time, she looked over at her mother in the stands, clapping proudly. If only George and her father were here to see this. When Millie returned her focus to the dugout, she saw coach at the far end of the fence talking to Mr. Green.

Central High scored a run in their half of the third inning—highlighted by a key sacrifice bunt by Millie. She returned to the mound to start the fourth inning with a score of 1-1. She was almost done with her warmup pitches when coach emerged from the dugout. He sauntered out to the mound, where he was met by Grogan.

"That's good, kid," he said, holding out his hand for the baseball. "We're gonna hand it over to Green." Over Coach Shellman's shoulder, Millie saw Johnny Green step out of the dugout and lumber to the mound.

Millie was speechless, and, for once, so was Grogan. She handed the ball to coach and walked towards to dugout with her head down. She didn't realize it until she was walking down the steps, but the crowd was on their feet for a standing ovation.

Coach returned to the dugout, keeping his distance from Millie. She was somewhat satisfied, watching him seethe when Johnny Green couldn't throw a strike. The County All-Stars scored five runs before he recorded an out and nine before the inning was over. Central High never recovered, losing 13-2. It would have been more had it not been for some spectacular plays by Edwards. He also provided River Junction's only other run with a majestic home run over the scoreboard in left field.

After the game, coach let the team sit in silence down the left field line. When he finally addressed them, he said very little. "I thought we were more prepared than that," he said, kicking the ground. "Let's take the rest of the week off, enjoy the holiday, and come back fresh next Monday."

CHAPTER

Millie's performance, once again, garnered special recognition from the *River Junction Review*. The headline read: "County All-Stars outlast Millie's Moxie." A cartoon accompanied it of her and George playing catch from halfway across the globe. Underneath it read: "The Bauer kids having a toss."

The week off was a relaxing one for Millie. With no baseball in the morning, she slept in past eight, but the following Monday, Millie's eyes shot open. She jerked her head in the direction of the clock, which read 8:05. She had overslept!

Within minutes of waking, she was halfway to Badger Park, working up a sweat as she jogged. Cresting the Popple Avenue hill, she saw the team was stretching.

She picked up her pace, using the grade of the hill to her advantage.

When Millie got to the park, she tried to sneak into the back row of the stretching lines, but coach called her out.

"Come on over here, Bauer," he said, making his way to the elm tree.

By now, Millie had come to know that good things seldom happen when coach wanted to talk under the old elm. She tried to catch the eye of one of her teammates to give her some razzing, but all of them kept their faces to the ground or made an exaggerated point of not looking in her direction.

"Sorry, Millie, but for now, you're off the team," said coach, cutting to the chase.

"It was an accident, coach." pleaded Millie. "I won't be late again."

"No, no, it's not that, Bauer," replied coach. He extended his hand and gave Millie's shoulder a firm yet comforting shake. "I can't go into it right now, but it's not my decision."

Millie rapidly blinked, fighting back the tears. "What did I do, coach?"

"Nothing, Bauer," said coach. He took off his hat and ran his hand through his crew cut. "You did everything I asked and more."

"Will I be able to play again?" she asked.

"Like I said, for now, you can't practice or play with the team," replied coach.

Still somewhat out of breath, a shell-shocked Millie dejectedly trudged towards home. She reached into her pocket and clutched the telegram. Playing baseball had been her major distraction from worrying about George. Approaching the library, she decided to stop in to read the newspaper. In her haste to leave the house, she wasn't able to check for his name.

When she got to the periodicals room, Millie saw that someone else was reading the *Review*. She decided to go look at an atlas to see if she could figure out where George was. Leaving the room, Millie nearly walked right into Lieutenant Baxter from the train station.

"Excuse me," said the Lieutenant. She then looked at Millie with a furrowed brow, trying to place her face. With her overalls and ball cap on, Millie looked much different from the day they met.

"Excuse me, ma'am," said Millie, who put her head down and headed for the exit.

"Millie?" said the Lieutenant behind her. "Millie Warren?"

Millie didn't turn around. Once outside, she ran down the steps and headed back up the Popple Avenue Hill, heading for High Point Cemetery.

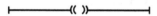

Millie silently entered the large black iron gates of the cemetery. She ran towards her father's headstone, past large mausoleums built for lumber barons and unmarked pauper graves. Millie and her mother used to come to the cemetery almost daily. They talked aloud to him and asked his advice. Now, Millie couldn't even recall the last time she was here. Finally, she came to his gravesite, collapsing out of breath. Exhausted, she slid into the shade behind the headstone, lying in silence, thinking about what just transpired.

Millie had no idea how long she had been sitting there. She groggily made her way out of the cemetery towards home. Turning the corner of her street, Millie saw coach's truck parked in front of her house. As she walked up the driveway, coach emerged from behind the shed along with, of all people, Paul Warren.

"Where have you been, Bauer?" asked coach.

"Does it matter?" snapped Millie. She was still raw from being dismissed from the team.

"Listen, Millie," said coach. "I'm just as sick about this as you."

"Who was it, Coach?" said Millie. She could feel her emotions stirring again. "Mr. Green?"

"I can't name names," replied coach, "but the one doggone person in the park who didn't agree with you being on the mound has a lot of pull."

Millie knew it was Mr. Green. That's why coach had been talking to him at the fence.

"He demanded coach take you out before you took the mound," said Paul. "But coach wanted you to get a round of applause from the crowd."

"Enough, Warren," said coach. Though he acted upset, Millie could tell coach was happy Paul had said it.

"So, what are you two doing here?" asked Millie.

"Well, Bauer," said coach flipping a ball to Millie. "I want you to continue on a pitching routine, and I want Warren here to be your catcher."

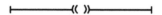

The next morning, Paul knocked at Millie's door with full catcher's regalia in hand. "Ready to go?" he asked excitedly.

"I'll meet you out by the shed," she replied.

Once they began playing catch, Millie noticed a difference in Paul. She wasn't sure if she was imagining it, but he looked like he was starting to get a little taller and thinning out. Not only that, but he was even able to throw a couple in a row to her. It was much different from weeks earlier when they had played catch at the sandlot.

With all that had been going on, Millie had stopped seeking out ball games around town, while Paul seemed to be getting better by playing at the lots.

Paul still had lapses in his skills, though, sending a few balls sailing over Millie's head into the Victory Garden.

On one such occasion, Millie was walking back to the mound when she saw the mailman walking up the sidewalk.

"Mail break," she shouted, dropping the ball and mitt and sprinting for the back porch.

Paul got out of his crouch with a groan and gingerly took off his catcher's equipment.

"Pour me a glass of lemonade, will ya?" he shouted to Millie in a parched voice.

Millie tore through the kitchen and dining room to the front hallway. On the floor was a pile of mail. Off to the side was a large envelope.

By now, Millie had trained herself to sort through the letters before looking at a larger parcel. She breezed by the four letters addressed to her mother before flipping over the manila envelope. Millie's eyes shot up to the envelope's upper left corner, which read, "Minneapolis Millerettes."

Millie carefully opened the envelope and pulled out a letter. As she unfolded it, several pieces of paper fluttered to the ground. Among them, she could see vouchers for train tickets on the Twin Cities 400. She read the letter with trembling hands.

Dear Ms. Bauer,

As a member of the All-American Girls Professional Baseball League, the Minneapolis Millerettes baseball club is always seeking talented girls to fill our roster. Your name comes highly recommended by Mr. Orville Shellman, coach at River Junction Central High. We are extending an invitation for you to travel to Minneapolis on Friday, July 14, to try out for a spot on the Millerettes at Nicollet Park. Following the tryout, you will be our guest when the Millerettes play the Milwaukee Chicks.

Enclosed are two train vouchers and game tickets for yourself and a guest if you desire to bring one. A chaperone will meet you at the train station if you wish to attend and will be your guide for the day. We also highly recommend that you read the pamphlet we have sent. "A Guide for All American Girls" spells out the league's conduct policy for all girls.

The Minneapolis Millerettes ball club hopes that you accept our invitation, and we look forward to seeing you on the field. If you do plan on coming, please bring appropriate baseball clothes.

Sincerely,

Bubber Jonnard
Manager
Minneapolis Millerettes

Shocked, Millie walked into the kitchen holding the letter and envelope.

Paul was helping himself to a glass of lemonade. He stood up straight when he saw Millie holding the envelope. He wiped his mouth with the back of his hand before speaking, "Something from George?"

"Um, no," Millie had momentarily forgotten about her initial reason for pillaging the mail.

"Who is it from then?" he inquired, walking over to Millie.

Without a word, Millie handed the letter over to Paul, who then began reading the letter. The only sound in the room was his heavy breathing.

"Holy moly, Millie!" said Paul incredulously, his voice rising a few octaves. "They want you to go up to Minneapolis to try out!"

Millie stood speechless, her mouth agape.

"Are you going to go?" asked Paul excitedly.

"Should I?" said Millie, taking back the letter and envelope. She couldn't believe she was asking Paul Warren for advice. "That's only three days away."

"Jeez, Millie," he replied. "I think you'd be crazy not to!"

Millie just stared blankly, dumbfounded by the situation.

"I think you better bring your personal catcher," said Paul.

CHAPTER

Three days later, Millie and Paul stood in silence on the train station platform, bags by their feet, waiting for the Twin Cities 400. Millie had read *A Guide for All American Girls* twice over the last few days. She concluded that the All-American Girls Professional Baseball League expected their players to dress as if they were Cinderella when they were in public. So she decided it was best if she wore her Sunday dress and applied what makeup she could without looking like a clown. Paul wore his Boy Scouts uniform.

"Did you ever talk to your mother about going?" asked Paul, breaking the silence.

"No," replied Millie. She had thought about it, but with how secretive both of them were being, she figured, what would be one more secret?

"Where did you tell her you were going?" asked Paul.

"I didn't tell her anything," said Millie. "She was gone before I even got up this morning."

"I told my parents I was taking the bus up to Timber Point to spend the day at Chippewa Park," said Paul.

The pair suddenly realized they weren't supposed to be there. They looked around to make sure no one they knew was at the depot.

Before long, the train pulled up to the platform.

"If the chaperone doesn't show up, I know how to get to Nicollet," bragged Paul, climbing aboard the train. He spoke with the confidence of a season ticket holder, not the person who had gone to one Minneapolis Miller game a few years ago. Millie was supposed to have gone to that game with Paul, Art, and George, but she had a really bad sunburn and stayed home.

Millie didn't respond. She was certain the chaperone would be there waiting. From what she read in the *Guide*, players didn't go anywhere without one.

They rode in silence in the coach car. Millie stared out the window, taking in the beautiful western Wisconsin countryside. Paul had his nose buried in his *Boy Scout Handbook*.

Finally, Millie turned towards Paul. "Why did you agree to come over to my house and catch me?"

"Because coach said if I keep working at it, I might be able to actually play someday," said Paul with a wistful look in his eyes.

Millie simply nodded. She thought of the work they had put in these last few days. They spent several hours in the hot sun, with Millie practicing her underhand softball delivery. She threw from 40 feet—the designated distance for the league—and it wasn't easy. The first day she threw ball after ball over Paul's head and in the dirt, leaving him bruised, but he never complained. Finally, yesterday, she started to find a pitching rhythm.

Paul continued, breaking Millie's thoughts. "He said that catching you might give me a leg up."

"Well, we'll have to keep working together then," said Millie with a smile.

"That would be great," replied Paul gratefully.

"I can't believe we are going to be on the same field that Ted Williams played on!" he said excitedly.

"Me, too," said Millie with a nod.

Millie turned back towards the window, getting lost in her thoughts. Not a word was spoken between the two for the rest of the trip. Questions swirled in her head as the lush green fields flew by. *Was George alive? What was her mother up to? Would things be different if her father were still alive?*

Paul couldn't contain his excitement. He talked to anyone who made eye contact with him. He tried weaving in a conversation what they were going to do, but when Millie gave him an icy glare, he changed the subject to scouting and some of his upcoming service badges.

Before Millie knew it, the train was crossing the Stone Arch Bridge, pulling into Minneapolis' Great Northern Depot. Millie thought of just telling Paul that they should get on the next train back to River Junction, but he was already halfway off the train before she could say anything.

When Millie stepped off into the depot, she saw a woman she was certain to be the chaperone, along with a younger woman. They spotted Millie and walked towards her. The women were impeccably dressed, with flawless hair and makeup.

"Ms. Bauer?" said the older woman, who looked to be Millie's mother's age.

"Yes, ma'am," replied Millie.

"I'm Ms. Fontaine," she said, shaking Millie's hand gracefully. "So glad you decided to come. This is Dottie Wiltse," gesturing to the woman that accompanied her. "She is a pitcher for the Millerettes."

"Nice to meet you both," said Millie shaking their hands.

"I'm Paul Warren, Millie's personal catcher," said Paul, awkwardly butting in.

Ms. Fontaine and Dottie were just as gracious to him as they were to Millie. "How do you do, Mr. Warren?"

"Swell!" he responded gleefully.

"Why don't we get over to the park," said Ms. Fontaine. "We'll grab a bite to eat, and then you can go through your workout."

"I like your dress, Ms. Bauer," said Ms. Fontaine as they made their way to a streetcar. "I see you must have read the pamphlet we sent over."

"Yes, ma'am," said Millie, nodding.

Millie, Paul, Ms. Fontaine, and Dottie chatted throughout the whole streetcar ride over to Nicollet Park. Millie's nerves were growing, but luckily Paul did most of the talking, bragging on her behalf. Both Ms. Fontaine and Dottie were politely attentive in their listening and reactions to his stories.

Finally, they reached the corner of Nicollet and 31st Street, across from Nicollet Park. A banner above the entrance read, "Minneapolis Millerettes vs. Milwaukee Chicks, today at 6:00."

"Dottie will take you to the locker room to eat and then change," said Ms. Fontaine. The foursome crossed the street and entered the stadium.

"I'll make sure Paul gets fed and then a tour of the park," she said before they parted ways.

"So, I hear you were playing with the high school baseball team," said Dottie while they ate the ham sandwiches that were waiting for them in the locker room.

"Well, I pitched in one game," said Millie. It was the most words she had spoken since they left the train station.

"Still, that's pretty remarkable," replied Dottie, truly impressed.

"If you don't mind me asking," said Millie. "How did you end up playing here?"

"Well, long story short, I was invited to a tryout at Washington Park in Chicago," said Dottie in a tone that conveyed she had told the story before. "When it was over, me and three girls from California were shipped to Minneapolis."

"California….wow," replied Millie. It seemed like another planet. "Do you get homesick?"

"Sometimes," said Dottie. "But we have a great group of girls, and we always have a lot of fun both on the field and off."

This time it seemed like it was a statement that she had practiced.

"Well, you better get changed, Millie; they are expecting you on the field in a few minutes," said Dottie, leaving the room. "And, remember, just think of it as if you were playing in your backyard." It was the first time Millie thought Dottie wasn't saying something she was told to.

Millie's metal spikes echoed on the concrete as she walked alone from the clubhouse to the dugout. The butterflies in her stomach danced with each step.

She was greeted in the dugout by Paul, sitting alone, cross-legged, talking to a man dressed in full catcher's equipment. "Looks like you get to throw to a major league catcher," said Paul, nodding towards the man.

"Thanks for coming over to try out," said the man, springing up from the bench and greeting Millie. "Clarence Jonnard, but everyone calls me 'Bubber.'"

"Millie Bauer," replied Millie. "Nice to meet you, Mr. Jonnard."

"Call me, Bubber," he said with a smile and a nod. "Let's get started, Ms. Bauer."

"Paul, why don't you be my bench coach and let me know if you see anything from this angle," directed the coach.

"Sure," replied Paul. He didn't realize it was a ploy to have him stay out of the way.

Millie and Bubber stepped out of the dugout and began playing catch parallel to the stands.

"So, Shell tells me you've got some dandies in that arm of yours," said Bubber.

"Sometimes," said Millie. "Coach has been a huge help for that."

"He told me you were modest," replied Bubber. "But, the truth is, you can't teach talent, kid."

Millie and Jonnard spent a while talking about the technique of throwing the ball underhand. For all that Paul had done for her, it helped to get a few pointers from Bubber. He said that League officials had just started using a smaller ball, so he showed her a few different grips for getting a good spin on it. He was surprised at how long Millie's fingers were, which gave her a definite advantage.

"We are going to throw 25-30 pitches and see what you have," said Bubber. "Then I'll see how you field your position."

Jonnard retreated behind the plate, spit in his catcher's mitt, rubbed it in, and pulled the catcher's mask over his face. "Let's see what ya got, lefty," he said, getting into a crouch.

Millie focused on the mitt, went into her whirlwind windup, and let it fly. Bubber didn't even move. The ball sailed over his head, hitting three-quarters up the backstop. The second it left her hand, Millie knew it was bad. She looked skyward and wiped her left hand on her pant leg.

Jonnard lifted his mask and looked over at Paul. "What did you think of that one?"

"Just missed," said Paul, not skipping a beat.

Jonnard retrieved the ball and jogged it out to Millie. "Nice and easy," he said, placing the ball in Millie's glove. "It's just you and me playing catch here, Lefty." He retreated behind the plate and repeated his routine. Once again, he spit in his mitt, rubbed it in, pulled down his mask, and gave a whistle as he got in his crouch.

Millie repeated her windup, but this time she barely felt the ball leave her hand. The result was a perfect toss, curving over the plate at the last possible second. She felt the tension leave her body.

"All right," said Jonnard snapping the ball back to Millie. "Now repeat that same motion."

Millie did just that, throwing the next 23 pitches fluidly. Bubber barely had to move his mitt.

"I would have brought my rocking chair out if I had known you could pitch like that," said Jonnard when they were done. "Say, just out of curiosity, why don't you step on back to the big mound? Shell piqued my curiosity about what you can do with the hardball."

"What about the fielding drills?" asked Millie.

"No need," said Bubber, "Schucks, I'd sign you right now if I could, kid, but 'cause of your age, we gotta have someone sign off on it."

Millie wondered what her mother would say if she knew she was over here without her permission.

"You mean my mother has to agree to me playing ball?" asked Millie.

Bubber nodded and then turned his attention towards the dugout. "Hey, Paul," shouted the coach.

"Why don't you grab a baseball and come and catch Ms. Bauer?"

Paul nearly fell on his face jumping to the request. Once behind the plate, he was nearly flawless, too. Even his throws back to Millie were on the mark. "Looks like we got ourselves a regular Bill Dickey here," said Jonnard, referring to the great New York Yankees catcher. Millie could see the catcher's mask lift on Paul's face from his broad grin.

"That's good," said Jonnard after he had seen enough. "Why don't you two grab a prime seat and enjoy the game."

"So when should we hear something?" asked Paul.

Jonnard threw his head back and laughed. "Looks like you got yourself a promoter there, too, Ms. Bauer."

Millie rolled her eyes.

Jonnard pulled out some money and gave them each a few dollars. "The hot dogs are pretty darn good."

"Thank you," they said in unison.

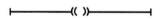

Paul and Millie watched the game from behind home plate. There were maybe a few hundred people in the stands as the Millerettes eked out a 7-6 win over the Chicks. Both were impressed with how skillful the girls played the game, especially the pitcher Dottie Wiltse, who had met them at the station. Millie couldn't imagine playing in the uniforms—a one-piece dress with tight shorts underneath and knee-high socks. Furthermore, she couldn't fathom wearing lipstick on the ball diamond.

It was nearly midnight when they made it back to River Junction.

"What are you going to tell your parents?" asked Millie as they walked out of the depot.

"I'll just tell them we had a big secret project up at the park," replied Paul. "How about you?"

"I don't think my mother will even know I was gone," said Millie dejectedly.

She was right. Millie arrived home to an empty house.

CHAPTER

Millie now had two pieces of mail to anticipate, but each day was disappointed when rifling through the pile. She continued her practice sessions with Paul, too, but as the days progressed, she threw less and less from the All-American Girls Professional Baseball League distance, returning to the longer regulation baseball mound.

Coach Shellman stopped by on Friday to make sure that Millie was still throwing. "I talked to Bubber, and he said that he was really impressed by your workout," said coach, standing behind Millie and watching her pitch.

"Not impressed enough to send me a contract, though?" Millie snapped.

"Listen, Bauer," said coach. "Bubber's hands are tied. There are a few things going on in Minneapolis that are keeping him from signing you."

Millie didn't speak. She reared back and tossed a fastball that popped in Paul's mitt.

"Bubber knows pitchers," said coach. "Heck, he's seen and caught some of the best. He said one of the toughest to catch was Clarence Mitchell, a left-handed spitballer. When he saw the natural movement on your pitches from the big mound, he thought you were throwing a spitter."

Millie's anger subsided. She wondered if what coach said was true. He had never lied to her before.

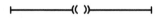

Nearly two weeks after her tryout with the Millerettes, Millie was given the answer to one of the questions when she opened the newspaper to the sports section. "Millerettes Lost to Minneapolis for the Rest of the Year," read the headline, followed by a brief article.

Due to a lack of fan interest, the Minneapolis Millerettes have canceled the remainder of their home dates for the 1943 season. They will play out the duration of their schedule away from Minneapolis.

Millie was disappointed, but wasn't sure that her mother would have allowed her to sign with them anyway. She didn't have much time to think about it. Almost on cue, Paul knocked at the back door for their workout. She showed him the article. He seemed unfazed by the news.

"That doesn't mean they don't want you to play for them," he said, urging Millie to get her glove and head out by the shed.

"Not today, Paul," said Millie. "I'm just not feeling up to it."

"Come on, Millie," replied Paul. "Coach is going to be calling me and asking how the workout went."

Millie wished her mother was here to shoo away Paul from the back door like a stray cat. Millie hadn't been sleeping well, and with the news about the Millerettes, she wasn't sure she should even go on with the daily workouts with Paul.

"Why don't we do it this afternoon?" she said, unsure if she would actually want to later.

Paul huffed and puffed but finally agreed. "Fine, but you better be ready to pitch then."

"Don't worry, I will," she said, closing the door before finishing her sentence. She heard him stomp down the steps muttering to himself.

Millie walked into the living room and plopped down on the couch with a sigh. She read the article a few more times and drifted off to sleep. An hour later, Millie was awoken by the mail slot slamming shut. There was only one piece of mail on the floor, a rarity. Millie trudged over to the lone letter and picked it up. The letter was addressed to: "Guardian of Ms. Mildred Bauer." The return address was:

P.K. Wrigley
Wrigley Building
401 North Michigan Ave.

Dear Ms. Bauer,

Based on your performance at the tryout with Bubber Jonnard, we are offering you a contract with the

*Minneapolis Millerettes for the duration of the 1944 All-
American Girls Professional Baseball League season.*

*Enclosed is a contract. Due to your age, we must have
a guardian sign the contract allowing you to join the
team.*

*If you have any questions, please call the Wrigley
Building at WB- 401000.*

Yours truly,

P.K. Wrigley

Millie wanted to show her mother, but she wasn't
sure whether she was at the factory or Armory. Instead,
she stuffed the envelope into her pocket alongside the
telegram, bolted out of the back porch, jumped on her
bike, and furiously pedaled towards Warren's Grocery &
Goods.

In minutes, Millie was bursting through the front
door, disrupting the quiet atmosphere inside the store.

"Millie," said a startled Mrs. Warren from behind the
counter. "Is everything okay, dear?"

"Yes, ma'am," said Millie, trying to catch her breath. "Is Paul around?"

"He just ran a delivery down the street. Is there something I can help you with?" inquired Mrs. Warren.

"No, I just wanted to talk to him about something important." Millie couldn't believe that she was so excited to tell Paul, but they had been working so hard together of late.

"Well, you can go relax in the backroom," suggested Mrs. Warren.

"Thank you, I'll do that, Mrs. Warren," said Millie, the burn finally leaving her lungs.

Art sat at the desk, his back to the door, looking over a ledger.

"I have something to show you, Art," said Millie.

Millie pulled out the contract envelope from her pocket to show him. Neither of them noticed the tattered, folded piece of paper that had fallen to the ground.

"This is from the Big Cheese himself," said Art incredulously.

Millie just stood there grinning.

"Paul told me about you two going up to Minneapolis, but I didn't believe him," continued Art. "Are you going to go for it?"

"I'm not sure," replied Millie. "I haven't mentioned it to my mother yet."

"Why not?" asked Art, perplexed.

"She has been so busy between work and going to the Armory to help at the infirmary that I haven't gotten a chance to talk to her," said Millie.

The sound of Paul's raspy voice came from the other room.

"I've got to tell Paul," said Millie, jumping to her feet and heading to the front of the store.

Paul was talking to his parents at the counter. She could barely contain her excitement while waiting for the conversation to end. He gave her a confused look as she smiled wildly.

Millie nearly jumped when Art tapped her on the shoulder. Millie spun around to see him, pale.

"You dropped this," said Art, holding out the frayed telegram in a shaking hand. He blinked back tears.

Millie's eyes widened.

"Let's go for a ride," said Art, turning and heading for the rear exit where his truck was parked. Millie followed silently.

As they got into the truck, Paul came running out behind them. "Hey, where are you going?"

"Scram," yelled Art.

"What's going on," said Paul with a confused look. Millie was beaming just a few minutes earlier, and now tears were rolling down her face.

"Go inside," ordered Art. "Tell ma I am taking Millie home."

"What about her bike?" asked Paul in a hurt tone.

Art didn't answer. He backed out and sped down the alley.

Millie and Art spent the next hour driving around town. She told him everything. She told him about the day the telegram arrived, how she kept it a secret from her mother, and how she worried every day that she would be found out. She also told him about her mother's odd behavior.

Art listened before finally speaking.

"Millie, I'm so sorry," he trembled. "But I was the one who dropped off the package that afternoon."

Millie's heart sank. It was one of her last hopes that George was still alive.

"George and I had worked it out months earlier," Art continued. "He had hoped he would be at the door delivering it to you, but in case he couldn't, he wanted to surprise you with the box."

"Thank you for doing that, Art," said a dejected Millie. "You meant…mean so much to George."

"So do you, Millie," replied Art, tears now streaming down his cheeks.

The two sat silently for the rest of the ride. When Art dropped off Millie, he reassured her. "Don't worry, Millie, your secret is safe with me."

"Thank you, Art," said Millie forcing a sad-eyed smile.

"And don't worry about Paul or my parents," he added. "I'll make up something for our hasty departure from the store."

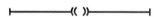

To distract herself, Millie worked in the Victory Garden but couldn't shake the despair she felt from Art learning her secret. He was one of the few people she knew would keep it between them, but the urge to tell her mother grew with each passing minute. She went inside to lay down and ponder the situation, but all thoughts in her head became muddled. Finally, Millie decided to go over to the Armory, where her mother was presumably working. She wanted to tell her everything.

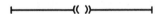

At the Armory, Millie approached the barracks apprehensively, wondering if she was doing the right thing. When she got to the door, she was met by a stoic soldier on guard duty.

"Can I help you, ma'am?" he asked.

"Is Helen Bauer here?" she probed.

"I'm sorry, ma'am, I can't tell you that," replied the soldier.

"Well, do you mind if I go in to find her?" asked Millie.

The soldier stepped aside and pointed at a red sign, which read: "Authorized Personnel Only." He said it aloud. "Sorry, ma'am. Authorized personnel only."

By now, Millie was thinking that maybe it wasn't time to tell her mother yet. "Thank you," she said, before going around the opposite side of the building from which she came. Turning the corner, she heard the sound of Bing Crosby crooning about Christmas.

Millie walked towards the far windows, where the music was coming from. She paused when she heard a familiar muffled voice. She looked around and pressed herself against the building.

When the music ended, Millie once again heard what she thought was her mother's voice. "I'm going to run this tray back to the cafeteria. You try to get some rest, dear."

Millie held her breath until she heard the door shut. She slowly moved along the wall, peeking around the corner of the window with burglar precision. She tried to peer in from the corner of her eye but saw nothing. The early evening sun made it impossible to look in. She cupped her hands on either side of her eyes to block out the glare and boldly pressed her face up to the window.

The first thing Millie saw were the legs of a person lying in a bed underneath the window. On the bedpost hung a white letterman's sweater, emblazoned with a large red "RJ." Her eyes darted wildly around the room. On the table sat a red scrapbook overflowing with newspaper articles. There was a familiar baseball jersey hanging from behind the door. On the wall was a picture of Bob Feller. A model airplane hung from the ceiling.

Pushing away from the window, Millie covered her mouth to quiet a scream. She turned around and ran home, not stopping until she was inside George's room. The scrapbook wasn't on the dresser. His sweater was missing from his desk chair. Millie didn't need to look any further. She fell onto George's bed and buried her face in his pillow. She let out a scream, one that had been building for weeks, and didn't stop until her voice was gone.

Retreating to her own bed, Millie lay paralyzed deep into the evening. Her mind began to play tricks on her. Maybe her mother brought those items in to tell the patient about George.

Around midnight, Millie heard her mother entering the front door. Millie's heart raced as her mother climbed the steps but, alas, never came in. Instead, under the door, she saw the light of George's room turn on across the hall, followed by the door closing. Ten minutes later, she heard his door open and close, followed by the sound of her mother locking it, before retiring to her own bedroom.

Millie was wide awake. In the years since George had enlisted, his room was rarely locked. She waited until she heard her mother's steady breathing. Quietly, Millie crept out of bed and walked across the hall. She tried the doorknob, which was locked. She then attempted to peer in through the keyhole, but the room was pitch-black. She knew she wasn't going to get to sleep without an answer.

CHAPTER 19

Millie took the side roads, unsure of what she would say if she ran into someone she knew or was stopped by the police. Approaching the barracks, Millie saw that very few room lights were on. For a moment, she was disoriented and couldn't remember which room it had been, but when she got closer, she was able to find the correct window. She quickly scanned the dark room and saw nothing. Out of the corner of her eye, she saw something hanging from the ceiling—a model airplane.

When she got home, she crept upstairs. She couldn't resist trying to get into George's room. Right as she was turning the doorknob, her mother appeared from her bedroom.

"Millie, what are you doing up at this hour, dear?" her mother asked blurry-eyed.

"I couldn't sleep, so I thought I'd look at George's scrapbook," she said. "Why is the door locked?"

Her mother perked up. "I must have locked it by accident. I am locking doors so often going in and out of rooms at the Armory that I must have done it by habit."

Millie stood in the hall waiting as her mother retrieved the key from her bedroom. When she confidently unlocked the door and opened it, Millie couldn't believe her eyes. George's letterman sweater hung from the chair at his desk. The picture of Bob Feller was again above his bed. On his dresser sat his bulging scrapbook. The only thing missing was the model airplane hanging from the ceiling.

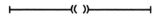

After a sleepless night, Millie had resigned to the fact that she was suffering some sort of mental breakdown. That was the only way she could describe it. She lay in bed until half-past eight when the aroma of frying bacon wafted up to her bedroom. Finally, a knock came at her bedroom door.

"Breakfast is served," said her mother, entering with a tray of food. Steam rose from the bacon and eggs. Glasses of orange juice and milk accompanied it.

"Don't you have to work today?" asked Millie.

"I took the day off to spend with you, dear," said her mother, setting they tray down next to the bed. She had barely sat down when the phone rang.

"I'll be right back," said Millie's mother, springing to her feet and out the door. The silhouette of her mother leaving the room looked oddly like what she saw — or dreamed of yesterday. Millie shook her head in hopes of wiping away that memory.

Minutes later, her mother remerged.

"Coach Shellman is coming over," she said with a curious look. "He wants to talk to us about something."

Mrs. Bauer left the room to tidy up for coach's arrival. Millie was finishing her breakfast just as coach was knocking on the front door. She put on her overalls and headed down to the kitchen, where her mother was pouring him a cup of coffee.

"Just the person I wanted to talk to," he said. He took a sip and then dove right into his reason for coming over. "Millie, I hear that Mr. Wrigley wrote to you."

"Who?" said Mrs. Bauer, nearly dropping the coffee pot.

There was no denying it. "Yes, coach," replied Millie.

"Why don't you go get the letter," directed coach, taking another sip and pursing his lips.

Millie retrieved the letter and bashfully stared at the ground while coach read the letter aloud.

"Please explain this, Mildred," said Mrs. Bauer.

Millie sat down and told the whole story. She thought her mother would chastise her, but she didn't.

"Is this really something you want to do, Millie?" asked her mother calmly.

"Yes," replied Millie.

"Well, then, let's give Mr. Wrigley a call," said her mother, matter-of-factly, as if she was calling down to the butcher shop.

Millie and coach huddled around Mrs. Bauer. After going through several connections, she finally got P.K. Wrigley on the line.

"Hello, Mr. Wrigley, this is Helen Bauer," said her mother.

"Yes, sir, that one."

"No, Mr. Wrigley, Mr. Bauer is deceased."

"Thank you, sir."

Millie could barely take the anticipation of only hearing half of the conversation.

"Coach, do you want to go out and throw the ball around?"

"Sure, kid," said Coach Shellman understandingly.

It seemed like forever before her mother came down the back porch steps.

"Well, Millie Bauer," said her mother. "I have some good news and some bad news."

"The good news is that you will be pitching for the Minneapolis Millerettes at the Western Wisconsin District Fair," said her mother with a smile.

Millie was speechless, her eyes widening.

"The bad news, Helen?" asked coach.

"The bad news," said her mother, pausing for effect. "The bad news is that you will have to buy a new dress for the meet and greet session."

All Millie could do was smile.

"I think we should go over to *Butler's*," said Mrs. Bauer.

Millie was dumbfounded by the series of events. To top it off, her mother suggested *Butler's Boutique*!

"Any interest in dress shopping, coach?" asked Mrs. Bauer playfully.

"I think not, Helen," said coach with a half-grin. "I forgot my purse at home."

"All right then, I'll go grab mine, and we can head out," said Mrs. Bauer returning to the house. "I think there might be a surprise for you later today, too."

Millie wasn't sure if she could handle any more surprises.

"Good for you, Bauer," said coach, lightly jabbing her shoulder. "You are going to go places in this game."

Millie heard the phone ring twice. Barely a minute had passed before her mother came running out of the house.

"I'm sorry, dear. There is an emergency over at the barracks," she said, frantically racing to the truck. "Millie, why doesn't coach drop you off at *Butler's*, and you can pick out a few dresses."

"Helen, are you sure about this?" asked a perplexed Coach Shellman.

Mrs. Bauer didn't answer, hopping in the pick-up and speeding off.

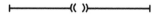

Millie had only window shopped at *Butler's*. It was a place where lawyers' and bankers' wives shopped.

"Can I help you, dear?" said the store clerk in a cold, unwelcoming tone.

"No, I'm just looking, ma'am," replied Millie, feeling out of place. She had no idea what she was supposed to be shopping for, but feigned interest in browsing amongst the racks.

"A special occasion, dear?" asked the woman persistently.

She was about to ask Millie to leave, when Mrs. Green, Johnny's mother, walked through the door. The store clerk turned all of her attention to the new customer. She ran into the back room and emerged with a seamstress, ready for Mrs. Green's beck and call.

"You should have called ahead, Mrs. Green," said the clerk, putting on a record. "Do you want me to close the store for a private showing?" motioning in Millie's direction. Classical music began playing from the phonograph in the corner.

"No, thank you, Jacqueline," said Mrs. Green, in an accent that didn't match her northern Wisconsin roots.

"I just need something to get my mind off Johnny and the worry he has caused me."

Millie's ears perked up. She remained in the corner with her back to the conversation.

"Oh my, what happened, if I so may inquire?" asked the seamstress in an overly concerned tone.

"Well," said Mrs. Green dramatically. "Johnny enlisted in the Marines."

Both women gasped. "Oh my!"

"Dare I ask, is he quite old enough?" piped in the store clerk.

"That doesn't seem to matter," said Mrs. Green.

Millie casually inched closer to the conversation, continuing to act like someone who was interested in clothes. Mrs. Green launched into her story. Apparently, after the July 4 game, Johnny had been very proud of his trumpet playing and, as always, was looking for his father's approval. Unfortunately, Mr. Green did nothing but berate him for his poor pitching performance. The argument came to blows, after which Mr. Green banished Johnny from the home. They had no idea of his whereabouts until they got a letter from him at Camp Pendleton in California.

Mrs. Green had to sit down because she had become so animated. The seamstress and clerk ran to get her a chair from the backroom. It was just Millie and Mrs. Green alone in the store. The clock's ticking seemed to be abnormally loud. Mrs. Green leaned against a counter, cooling herself with a hand fan.

For the first time, she acknowledged Millie's presence with a look of recognition. "Do I know you, young lady?" she asked Millie.

"Yes, ma'am," said Millie, surprised to be talking to Mrs. Green. "My name is Millie Bauer."

"*The* Millie Bauer," said Mrs. Green with a chortle. "My, my, my, has your name been mentioned a few times at our dinner table."

Millie could only imagine what Johnny, particularly his father, had to say about her.

Mrs. Green didn't seem interested in talking baseball with Millie. "What brings you down to Butler's, Ms. Bauer?"

"I'm supposed to be getting a dress for the Fair," replied Millie.

"Ah, yes, the Fair," said Mrs. Green with an air of superiority. "Have you found anything you like?"

"I'm not even sure where to begin, Mrs. Green," said Millie bashfully.

The two women reemerged from the back room. "Sorry we took so long, Mrs. Green," said the clerk, sliding a chair under the pampered customer and handing her a glass of something strong smelling.

"That's fine, ladies," said Mrs. Green, seemingly forgetting her discussion about her son. "I was just chatting with Ms. Bauer here."

The clerk gave Millie a disapproving look.

"Violet," said Mrs. Green to the seamstress. "Why don't you get Ms. Bauer's measurements? I'm going to pick out a few dresses for her."

CHAPTER

Millie should have been excited about the game at the Western Wisconsin District Fair, but she couldn't seem to shake feelings of doom. She still hadn't figured out whether she had dreamt of seeing her mother waiting on a soldier surrounded by George's belongings. She returned to the barracks a few nights in a row and was even bold enough to look in each window. Yet, there were no clues of what she had seen.

The daily sessions with Paul, which Millie had grown to enjoy, were also canceled. He was now working with the Boy Scouts, helping prepare the grounds for the Fair. She was supposed to be practicing during the week, but she spent most of the time lying on the couch, listening to the radio, and keeping an eye on the mail slot.

Good afternoon, ladies and gentlemen. This is Hugh Beatty reporting for WXOM Radio, broadcasting live from Timber Point at the Western Wisconsin District Fair.

I want to remind all of our listeners that we will be broadcasting from time to time throughout the day and evening, and our very own news broadcast at 5:45, starting today, August 8th, through Sunday, the 13th. For those of you in attendance at the fair, this is your chance to see in person how an actual radio broadcast is produced. Don't forget that our own program will be changed every day to bring you the greatest variety possible.

Millie could hear loud voices in the background.

Well, if you haven't already heard, today is Children's Day here at the fair. Now that the morning showers have come and gone, hundreds of youngsters have made their way along the fresh sawdust trail to the Midway, where the rides are spinning, and carnival barkers are in full throat.

I have with me a few of these young men and women who have already been tramping up and down the Midway. I want to hear what they are looking forward to.

"*What's your name, young lady?*"

"*Dorothy Jones.*"

"*Well, Dorothy, anything in particular that you are looking forward to?*"

"*Yes, sir, the 'Let Freedom Ring' show.*"

Ah, yes, "Let Freedom Ring" will go on each night through Saturday in front of the grandstands starting at eight, highlighted by vaudeville and circus acts, and ending with an exciting fireworks display.

Thank you, Dorothy.

And who are you, young man?

Andy Becker, sir.

What are you looking forward to?

I'm looking forward to the harness races and Doc Best's horror show.

Those are two of my favorites, Andy!

And in case you thought it was all fun and games for the young people, don't forget about those that are working here as well. The Boy Scouts are helping out with

*everything from traffic to security, and we have one right
here. What's your name, son?*

Paul Warren, sir.

Millie sprang up from the couch and turned the
radio up, eliciting a crackle.

*Mr. Warren, I know that you are all business when
you have the uniform on, but what are you looking
forward to?*

*Well, sir, I am looking forward to seeing Millie Bauer
pitch in the ball game on Saturday night between the
Minneapolis Millerettes and the Rockford Peaches.*

*Funny you should mention that, Paul, because just
moments ago, I was handed a poster for that ball game,
which will be broadcast live here on WXOM. Quite
a poster! It reads: 'Don't miss the chance to see River
Junction's own Millie Bauer try to throw them by the girls
from Rockford.'*

*Sounds like a peach of a game. Wish Ms. Bauer luck if
you see her, would you please, Paul?*

I will, but she doesn't need any luck.

Ha! Well, there you have it, folks.

*One more reminder before I sign off. In these war
times, I want to remind you that the Army, Navy, and*

*Marines, together with their women's organizations,
will all be represented on the grounds in the Merchants
Building. If the patriotic mood moves you, there will be
opportunities for enlistment.*

"That's it!" said Millie jumping up from the
couch. "If the patriotic mood moves you, there will be
opportunities for enlistment."

For the first time in weeks, Millie was confident in a
decision.

CHAPTER

The following evening at dusk, Millie was on a bus pulling into the Western Wisconsin District Fair parking lot. The familiar sounds and smells hit her the second she stepped off the bus. She walked through the entrance overwhelmed and went looking for the Women's Army Corp in the Merchants Building. Her condition wasn't helped by the fact that she had stayed up late into the night devising her plan—she was to join WACS and leave after her game on Sunday evening. She had thought about leaving before then, but her absence from the game would cause too many people to come looking for her right away.

Once inside the gates, Millie stopped to watch Andrews Sisters impersonators in their olive Army uniforms harmonizing on *Boogie Woogie Bugle Boy*. She couldn't help but think of Johnny Green when they sang:

> *He makes the company jump when he plays reveille.*
> *He's the boogie woogie bugle boy of Company B*

Johnny and his mother were one of the reasons that Millie stood there now. She was wearing one of the outfits Mrs. Green bought for her. It was like nothing she had ever worn before. Rather than the drab color and fabrics that most girls and women had adopted during the war, Millie wore a black skirt and a bright red blouse. She had also applied makeup the way that the women at Butler's had shown her. Even she was surprised at how much older she looked.

Millie quickly became self-conscious of her appearance when a few girls and a boy ran by, kicking up sawdust and hollering as they blazed a path up the midway. Millie looked towards the long corridor. She had intentionally wanted to avoid it, but it was difficult to resist. She was drawn by the carnival barkers and the constant loop of calliope music. The sound of laughter and yelling was too much for her to take.

"I'll just walk through, but I won't stop," she said aloud.

Memories flooded back when Millie entered the fairway, sawdust crunching under her feet. It had only been a few years since she was last there, but so much had happened between then and now. Her daydream was broken by the sight of a group of Boy Scouts. They were at the baseball toss, trying to knock aluminum milk jugs off a stool. She paused for a moment to make sure that Paul wasn't amongst them. She was aware that he would likely be at the Fair, but she didn't want to cross paths with him, especially with what she had planned.

Once she was sure Paul was out of sight, Millie moved closer to see if the boys were having any luck. By the way they were giving the thrower a hard time, it didn't look like any prizes were being won. The boy who just missed his last throw stepped back, red-faced, to let another one of them try. He glanced in Millie's direction and did a double-take. They looked at each other knowingly, but neither seemed to be able to place the other. Finally, she placed him.

"Ted?" Millie said.

The other boys turned to look. Millie recognized two of them. It was Ted, his brother Phil, and their friend, Tim, from the game of ball earlier in the summer.

"Yeah," he replied, still not sure who Millie was.

"It's Millie," she said.

It still took a few seconds for Ted to make the connection before a smile came across his face.

"Hey," said Ted excitedly. "It's Millie Bauer!"

Millie bashfully looked away.

"I didn't recognize you all gussied up," said Ted, adding to Millie's sheepishness.

"You excited for the game, Millie?" asked Phil, pointing to a poster hanging from the booth they were at.

Millie looked closer. It was the poster that Hugh Beatty described on the radio. She couldn't believe her eyes. She remembered it read: "Don't miss the chance to see River Junction's own Millie Bauer try to throw them by the girls from Rockford," but he failed to mention that there was a big picture of her in her windup. It looked like Mr. Christopher's handiwork.

The carnival barker looked over at the poster and then to Millie. "Ladies and gentlemen! Boys and girls!" he shouted at the top of his lungs. "Step right up and see the girl wonder, Millie Bauer, unleash her mercurial fling!"

A few people started to make their way over to the booth.

"Give it a try, Millie," said one of the other Scouts.

"I don't know," said Millie self-consciously.

"Come on, Millie," urged Ted. "I wanna see you knock em' down."

Millie rolled the sleeves up on her blouse and stepped up to the booth.

"Millie Bauer!" roared the barker.

"Millie Bauer!" mimicked one of the other boys.

People continued to congregate at the booth.

The barker handed Millie three balls and leaned in close. "This ones on me," he said in a voice not matching the one used to lure people to the stand. "Good luck, kid."

Millie focused in on the three milk jugs, wound up, and threw. Thud, the ball hit the canvas behind the jugs, which all sat perfectly in place on the stool. There were a few murmurs from the crowd. When the jugs were all intact after the second throw, even more groans came from the onlookers. Millie stepped back from the booth and took a deep breath. From the back of the group came a shout of encouragement, "Knock em' down, kid!"

A few more followed, "You can do it, Millie!"

"Show 'em what you got, Bauer!"

Millie returned to her spot and spun the ball in her hand. Focusing on the center of the jugs, she reared back and let a throw go with all her might. The jugs flew apart, bringing a loud cheer from the crowd. Millie exhaled.

"Millie Bauer!" shouted the barker to the crowd, who grew even louder.

"Come see her throw 'em by the Rockford Peaches tomorrow," he said, triumphantly holding up Millie's arm to the crowd.

Millie smiled and gave a slight wave to the onlookers. A few complimented her on their way by.

"That was keen, Millie," said Ted impressed.

"Thanks," replied Millie bashfully.

"We've been trying to knock those down for close to an hour!" continued Ted.

"Yeah, we thought he was trying to pull one over on us," added Tim.

"Well," said Millie after a few seconds of silence, remembering her reason for being at the fair. "I'm gonna get going."

"See you Sunday," said Ted cheerily.

Millie smiled and headed up the fairway towards the Merchant's building.

CHAPTER

Millie climbed the seven steps to the main hall of the Merchant's building. Inside, voices came from rooms, echoing down the halls. There wasn't anyone in the long corridor, but a lone Boy Scout, helping people with directions. Once he saw it was Millie, he went back to reading what looked like his *Boy Scout Handbook*.

The third door on the left was the Women's Army Corps room. A large poster sat on an easel outside the entrance. It had a picture of a female soldier with a flag behind her. It read: "Are you a girl with a Star-Spangled heart?"

Millie's pulse beat faster as she walked towards the door. She kept her head down, thinking about what she was going to say.

"Excuse me," said the Boy Scout from the end of the hall.

Millie came to a jolting stop. Her stomach lurched.

"Sorry, ma'am, no one is in there right now," he said. "They said to go ahead and look around. They'll be back in a few minutes".

Millie breathed easier. At least he thought she was old enough to call her "ma'am."

"Thank you," she replied.

Millie only made it a few feet into the room when she was overcome with patriotism. She was certain she was making the right decision. There were posters covering the walls showing different jobs that women were doing in the Army. There were nurses, typists, cooks, radar specialists, translators, drivers, telephone operators, and radio intelligence officers.

Under the pictures were tables with all the uniforms that WACS soldiers were issued. In the corner was a spread of brochures. Millie walked to the table to inspect the various outfits.

"Ma'am," a voice came from behind her.

Millie spun around to see a woman dressed in military-issued khaki.

"Hi, my name is Lieutenant Korum," said the smiling woman. "Do you have any questions?"

Millie was frozen. Her eyes darted around the room. She tried to remain calm, remembering what she had planned to say.

"Um, yes," she said with a quiver in her voice.

"Excellent. What can I help you with?" replied the Lieutenant.

Before Millie could reply, a familiar raspy voice came from behind the Lieutenant. "Millie?"

The Lieutenant turned around, revealing Paul standing in the doorway in his Boy Scout uniform.

"Hi, Paul," said Millie, trying to sound cheerful.

"What are you doing in here? Trying to sign-up?" he said with a grin, unaware that was exactly what she was doing.

In an instant, Millie's plan had been spoiled by the appearance of Paul. She tried to force a smile. "Oh, um, I was wondering if there was anything that we could do as teenagers."

"How old are you?" asked the Lieutenant.

"Fourteen, ma'am," replied Millie.

"Really," said the woman with a laugh, "I thought you were actually here to enlist."

Millie's heart sank. "No, ma'am."

"There are plenty of things that children can do to support the war effort at home," replied the Lieutenant, launching into a sales pitch.

Millie didn't hear any of it. She stood fixated on Paul, who had unknowingly foiled her plan.

When the Lieutenant finished, Paul excused himself from the conversation to relieve the Boy Scout at the end of the hall from his post, but not before telling the woman about Millie pitching in the game on Sunday.

Millie lingered in the room for a few minutes before exiting.

"Good luck!" said the Lieutenant cheerily.

"Thank you, ma'am," replied a crestfallen Millie.

Millie glanced with contempt at Paul, who had his nose buried in the *Boy Scout Handbook*. He looked over the top of it at her with a smile.

"Are you all set for Sunday?" he asked.

All Millie could do was nod *yes* before heading for the door. She needed to get outside to the fresh air. Paul called her name a few times, but she didn't turn around to answer.

Outside, Millie felt the ground shaking. No one else seemed to be feeling the tremors. She made a dash for the parking lot, where she hopped on the next bus back to River Junction, her head spinning.

The sick feeling that had overtaken Millie at the fair subsided on the ride between Timber Point and River Junction. Stepping off the bus, she breathed deeply, taking in the comfortable night air. Millie wasn't sure what she was going to do now that her plan to join the Women's Army Corps was dismantled. By the time she got home, she had decided that maybe things would work out for the best. Rather than be concerned about leaving for basic training, she could focus on the game tomorrow.

At peace with her decision, Millie walked around the house. She glanced over at the Victory Garden. Though it was pitch black out, she could see that the lack of tending to over the past few weeks had led to weeds sprouting up throughout.

Millie walked up the back porch and entered the dark house. When she flipped on the light, Millie was surprised to see a package on the kitchen table with a note next to it. She picked up the piece of paper. It was from her mother.

Millie,

This arrived around supper time this evening. I didn't open it, but I'm assuming it's for your game tomorrow.

Millie glanced at the address, which read: "Wrigley Building 401 North Michigan Ave.," then back at the letter.

Millie, I am so proud of you and all that you have accomplished this summer. I realize that we haven't seen each other much, but I hope that will change shortly. I will try desperately to get to the game tomorrow night, but if I don't, please know that I will be listening to the game on the radio and know that your father and brother will be with you in spirit.

Love,

Mom

Millie was so exhausted from the day that she wasn't upset that her mother wasn't sure if she would be able to attend the game. However, she did feel a twinge of loneliness when her father and George were mentioned. She opened the box to find a Millerettes uniform, hat, and stockings inside, with a note to be at the fair by four o'clock. They also wanted her to dress as instructed in *A Guide for All American Girls.* She left the contents in the box on the table and shuffled off to bed.

CHAPTER

Coach Shellman came by the house around noon to give Millie some words of encouragement. He coaxed her into going out to the tannery shed for some throws. It had been a few days since Millie practiced her underhand throwing, but after a few pitches she was hitting coach's mitt wherever he placed it.

"Looks good, kid," said coach, wiping the sweat from his brow.

"You going to be there, coach?" asked Millie.

"Wouldn't miss it for the world," replied coach with his familiar half-grin.

"Thanks," said Millie, forcing a smile.

"Is Helen, I mean, your mother going to be there?" he asked.

"I hope," she said, looking down at the ground and moving the dirt side to side with her feet.

Coach lifted her chin so that their eyes met. "Whether she is there or not, your mother loves you very much, Millie."

Tears came to Millie's eyes.

"Your father and brother would be very proud of you, too," he continued, his voice quivering. He leaned in and hugged her.

"Say, how 'bout I give you a ride up to the fair?" said coach, patting Millie's head. "I wanted to get there a little early and talk to Bubber."

"That would be great, Coach," replied Millie wiping tears from her eyes.

"I'll be here around three," he said.

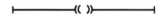

The ride to the Western Wisconsin District Fair was a relatively peaceful one. Millie wore the same outfit as the night before, not brave enough to venture from the black skirt and red blouse. Heading north in coach's old truck, he told Millie stories about him and Bubber Jonnard playing together for the Nashville Sounds in the Southern Association. Millie closed her eyes, letting the breeze blow in her face. She didn't want the moment to end.

They pulled into the parking lot just as the Millerettes bus arrived. A man stepped off first and stretched. Millie recognized him. It was Jonnard. Her view of him was quickly blocked by a parade of women who looked like they were heading for a beauty contest. The last one out was their chaperone, Ms. Fontaine.

"Bubber," shouted coach over toward the bus.

Jonnard looked around to see where the voice was coming from.

"Bub," coach shouted again, waving.

Millie and coach got out of the car and walked toward the group. Coach and Bubber shared a hearty handshake, their forearm muscles flexing in the embrace.

"Ms. Bauer," said Bubber, nodding in her direction before he and coach stepped to the side to converse.

"Millie," said Ms. Fontaine. "I love your outfit. Did you receive your uniform?"

"Thank you, yes I did, Ms. Fontaine," replied Millie bashfully.

"Why don't you come meet the girls," said the chaperone, beckoning Millie over.

Millie was welcomed with open arms by the girls. They all seemed very happy that she would be joining them for the game. Millie was reliving her triumph of the baseball toss from the night before with a few of the girls when coach came up to her. "Sorry to interrupt," he said, looking agitated. "I need to talk to you, Bauer."

"Um, sure, coach," said Millie confused.

"Sorry, ladies," he said to the girls. He and Millie walked a distance from the group.

"Millie, I'm not sure when you are going to get a fair shake," he said, gritting his teeth.

Millie looked at coach, unsure of what he meant.

"Did Mr. Green do something?" said Millie, trying to lighten coach's mood.

Coach forced a smile and snorted. "No, it sounds like they were using you."

"What do you mean," she replied, growing concerned. "Am I not going to pitch?"

"Yes, you are, but only for an inning," he said, red in the face. "I guess they're gonna be playing on the road from here on out. Gonna be called the Orphans or something like that. They need ways to sell tickets, and having attractions like you is one of those ways."

"Well, I'll just pitch my best for that inning then," said Millie optimistically.

"With all that you have been through," said coach shaking his head. "I'd like to see you get a whole outing."

"Maybe someday," Millie continued. She could see Bubber watching them.

"What did Mr. Jonnard say?" She asked.

"He's not too happy about it, but it came from Mr. Wrigley," said coach. "He wanted to tell you himself, but I insisted I pass along the news to you."

"Thanks, coach," said Millie, "for everything."

"Doggone it if you aren't going to be pitching for me next year, kid," said coach shaking his heading

"Attention, ladies," shouted Jonnard, motioning the team over. "Ms. Fontaine has an addendum to the itinerary."

The team gathered around Ms. Fontaine. "Well, ladies, we don't need to change on the bus today," said the chaperone with a smile. "The good people at the fair have given us part of the Administration Building to use as a locker room. Remember to thank the staff."

Millie saw the relief on many of the girls' faces. They must have been dressing on the bus of late.

"Now, let's go get changed, ladies," continued Ms. Fontaine. "We have to be on the field by 4:45 for a meet-and-greet."

The team got a lot of looks as they made their way to the Administration Building. The girls hastily dressed and freshened up their make-up. A few assisted Millie, making sure she was up to standard. The last thing she did was tuck the telegram inside the brim of her cap.

Ms. Fontaine pulled Millie aside as the team was exiting the building. "Say, Millie. WXOM requested an interview with you," she said.

"Um, all right," replied Millie, watching her new teammates file towards the field.

"I'll walk you over the radio tent," said Ms. Fontaine in a reassuring tone.

She reminded Millie to mind her manners. "Remember," she said to Millie, "Emily Post says 'charm cannot exist without good manners.'"

Millie and Ms. Fontaine politely worked their way through a large crowd that surrounded the radio tent until they came to a man that Millie recognized as Hugh Beatty.

"Miss Bauer, I want to make you acquainted with Mr. Beatty," said Ms. Fontaine.

"How do you do?" said Millie, smiling and lightly bowing just as she was instructed. Ms. Fontaine smiled, pleased with Millie's étiquette.

"Nice to meet you, Miss Bauer," replied Hugh hastily. "We are going to be on in 15 seconds if you want to come take a seat."

Millie had barely sat down when Beatty launched into the broadcast.

Welcome back. This is Hugh Beatty, reporting live from the Western Wisconsin District Fair in Timber Point. There has been a whole lot going on here the last few days, with plenty to come.

Today's top act is being put on by the girls from the All-American Girls Professional Baseball League. This evening the Minneapolis Millerettes will try to defeat the Rockford Peaches. Should be one heckuva contest!

With me right now is one of the Minneapolis players, Millie Bauer, from River Junction. Welcome, Millie.

Thank you, Mr. Beatty. It's a pleasure to be here.

Millie, how does it feel to know that not only will all eyes be on you, but many ears will be listening to our live broadcast?

It's an honor to be in a Minneapolis uniform. I look forward to the challenge.

Tell me, Millie, how did you find your way onto the Millerettes?

Well, Mr. Beatty, I had a tryout at Nicollet Park in Minneapolis, and Mr. Wrigley contacted me a few weeks later.

Wow, that's quite an accomplishment for a girl just entering high school.

Thank you, sir.

Now, Millie, I have to ask. The Bauer name is familiar to a lot of people. Your older brother is George, am I correct?

Millie tensed up— her mouth went dry. She wasn't expecting a question about George.

Um, yes, sir. That is correct.

I know George is serving in the Army. Have you heard from him lately?

No, sir.

Hugh Beatty didn't see that Millie was losing the color in her face.

Maybe he heard about your exploits and is a tad jealous.

A loud roar of laughter came from the onlookers. Millie forced one herself.

Possibly.

Well, there you have it, Millie Bauer, the next star of the All-American Girls Professional Baseball League. If you can't make it up to the fair, make sure you tune into WXOM at six for the game. Thank you, Millie, and good luck.

Thank you, Mr. Beatty.

We'll be back with more from the fair in a few minutes.

Millie shook hands with Mr. Beatty and stepped away from the tent, sweating profusely.

"Well done, Millie," said Ms. Fontaine, beaming. "Let's head over to the field."

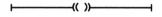

The minute Millie stepped onto the field she could tell that something was amiss. She started to warm up with the catcher, but one bounced ten feet in front of the girl and the next was launched ten feet over her head. Finally, Jonnard came over to her.

"Listen, lefty," said Jonnard, removing his cap to wipe his brow. "I want to start by saying that I'm sorry if you were misled by how much you would be playing today."

"Thank you, coach," replied Millie looking towards the nearly full grandstands.

"Now, I want you to know that I have the utmost confidence in your abilities," said Jonnard. "If you throw anything like you did in the Minneapolis tryout, you're going to be just fine."

Millie nodded.

"All right, kid, keep getting ready."

Millie continued to warm up, but it didn't get better.

Walking back to the dugout, she scanned the stands. Everywhere she looked, she seemed to know someone: Coach Shellman, Walter Edwards, Charlie Grogan, and the rest of the Central High team in their red ball caps. Mrs. Warren and Art were on their feet, clapping alongside a whole section filled with Boy Scouts, Paul's red hair sticking out. Millie even saw Mr. Green angrily chomping on a cigar, his attention directed at her. There was no sign of her mother.

Both teams lined up in the "V for Victory" formation. Millie's thoughts went to George while a member of the Boy Scouts played "The Star-Spangled Banner" on his bugle. She also thought about Johnny Green and what he was doing at this moment.

Apprehensively, Millie took the mound and started warming up. Nothing had changed. She felt helpless as every pitch ended up at the backstop.

Millie had never experienced this type of feeling on the pitcher's mound.

"Play ball," yelled the umpire.

What happened next was a blur. The first batter walked on four pitches. The last toss was the only one that made it into the catcher's mitt. Millie finally was able to get a pitch over the plate to the second batter, who laced it into the left-center gap for a triple. Millie walked the next two batters on eight pitches.

The catcher came out to try and calm Millie down, but it was to no avail. Millie's day finally came to an end when Jonnard emerged from the dugout. It was still the top of the first inning. The Peaches were leading 4-0, the bases were loaded, and no one was out.

Jonnard slowly walked to the mound, reaching out his hand for the ball. "There is gonna be a next time, kid."

Dejected, Millie walked off the field with her shoulders slumped. Through the applause she could hear Hugh Beatty: *A disappointing showing for Millie Bauer.*

People stopped by to offer encouragement: Coach Shellman, Walter Edwards, and Paul. Finally, when Mrs. Warren and Art came down, Millie couldn't contain her emotions. She choked back tears as Mrs. Warren's consoling words passed through the fence. For the next few innings, Millie milled about the dugout in a daze.

The Millerettes came back to win, 6-5. Dottie Wiltse came in as relief. She gave up a hit to the first batter she faced and then allowed only two more base runners—both on errors—the rest of the game.

After the game, Millie sat in the back of the group, hanging her head, while Jonnard addressed the team.

"Before we head to the locker room, I want to thank Millie Bauer for joining us," said Jonnard. "Despite what happened today, I think she has a bright future in this game."

The team turned to look at Millie, giving her a pleasant round of applause.

Millie quietly changed back into her skirt and blouse in the corner while the other girls chattered loudly. She thanked a few of them and then Ms. Fontaine before walking out of the building into the sounds of the fair.

Waiting for her was Coach Shellman. "Need a ride home, kid?" he asked.

"No, thank you, Coach. I'm gonna take the bus. I'll see you back in River Junction," said Millie as she walked towards the parking lot.

"Remember, Bauer," yelled coach from behind her. "You are going to be throwing for me next year."

CHAPTER

It was nearly 10 o'clock when the bus pulled into the station back in River Junction. Stepping off the bus, Millie breathed deeply, taking in the comfortable night air. She started toward home when out of the corner of her eye, a vehicle caught her attention. It was the WAC's recruiting car. Sitting inside was Lieutenant Baxter, who spotted Millie. She was out of the car and scurrying across the street before Millie could do anything.

Millie stopped walking.

"Millie Warren?" asked the Lieutenant catching her breath.

"Yes," said Millie, slipping back into the persona she had created at the train station weeks earlier.

"I've been trying to find you," said the Lieutenant, "but no one seems to have even heard of you."

Millie shrugged her shoulders. "I don't know many people."

Content with the answer, Lieutenant Baxter asked, "So, are you still interested in serving your country in the Women's Army Corps?"

"Yes, ma'am," replied Millie, looking around to see if anyone she knew was watching. The other passengers on the bus had dispersed. Lieutenant Baxter and Millie were alone on the sidewalk, and, but for the bus depot attendant, no one was in view.

"Why don't we get in my car and head over to the office," said the Lieutenant.

Things moved so quickly at the office that Millie barely had time to reconsider. She was surprised that Lieutenant Baxter asked few questions. When she did inquire Millie about her birth certificate, Millie told her it was lost.

"That shouldn't be a problem," replied the Lieutenant.

Nearly all the paperwork was finished. A bus voucher for 7 a.m. the next morning was in Millie's hand.

Right before Millie was going to sign her name, she had a second thought.

"I think I need to talk to my father," she blurted out.

"Are you sure, Millie?" asked Lieutenant Baxter. "This should be your decision."

"Yes, I'm sure," said Millie, abruptly standing up and heading for the door. She turned around and reassured the Lieutenant. "If everything goes well, I'll be here at six tomorrow morning with my bags packed."

Millie scurried home. She wanted to change into her overalls before she headed to the cemetery. When she turned the corner of her street, she saw Coach's truck in the driveway. Most of the lights were on in the house, including George's room. Millie began to turn around when a whistle pierced the night.

"Bauer!" shouted Coach Shellman.

Millie squinted to see coach standing on the front porch.

"I think you need to come home right now," said coach.

"Yes, coach," replied Millie.

Exhausted, Millie climbed the steps of the front porch. Looking past coach, she saw a military duffel bag sitting in the hallway.

"Is everything okay, Coach?" she asked, panicked.

"You'll need to go talk to your mother upstairs," he said stone-faced. "She's in George's room."

Millie cautiously climbed the creaky stairs, her knuckles whitening from gripping the railing. Her mother was sitting on George's bed, back to the door. Millie walked the last few steps and hesitated, preparing herself for the worst. She expected to find her mother on George's bed looking through his belongings, finally hearing about his missing in action status. Suddenly, she heard her mother laugh and then another laugh, one that she hadn't heard in some time.

Millie began to tremble. Once again, this time louder, the sound of laughter came from the room. It was unmistakable. It was George. She bolted into the room to see someone lying in George's bed, a pillow propped up behind him. In front of him was Millie's scrapbook. His face was badly scarred.

"Moxie," said the person, holding out their hand that had similar scars spider-webbing up his arm. The voice was George's.

Mrs. Bauer stood up and turned around. "Millie, isn't it great to have George back?"

Millie lunged towards the bed and fell to her knees. She wrapped her arms around George's waist and began to sob uncontrollably. Her brother stroked her hair as tears rolled down his cheeks.

Mrs. Bauer quietly backed out of the room and shut the door.

Other than gasping for air in attempts to compose themselves, the brother and sister sat in a silent embrace. A few times, they parted so that they could look each other in the eye.

Finally, Mrs. Bauer came back into the room. "Sorry, Millie," she said, resting a hand on Millie's shoulder. "George needs to get some rest."

Millie didn't want to let go of her brother.

"We'll talk in the morning, Millie," said George reassuringly. "You can tell me all about your exploits."

Millie gave George another tight squeeze and a kiss on his scarred cheek before walking out of the room.

Coach Shellman was standing halfway up the staircase. He smiled at Millie and nodded. Millie stepped out of the room, overcome. Coach saw the distress on her face and bolted up the remaining stairs and braced her before she collapsed. He assisted her over to the chair outside her mother's room. Millie looked towards George's room with a slight smile, shaking her head in disbelief.

Millie pulled the worn telegram out of her skirt pocket and handed it to her mother. Mrs. Bauer quickly scanned the document before handing it to Coach Shellman.

"Oh, Millie," she said. "Where did this come from?"

After composing herself, Millie told them about that last day of school when she was surprised at the door by the telegram delivery man. She told her about that night and how she watched her mother sleeping so soundly that she couldn't bear to tell her.

"Millie," her mother said, rubbing her daughter's cheek with the back of her hand. "It must have been a week later that I received a telegram stating that he was found and that he would be returning soon."

"I'll get some water, Millie," said coach retreating downstairs.

"Did coach know?" inquired Millie after he was gone.

"No," said her mother shaking her head.

"Did anyone else?" probed Millie.

"No one, Millie," said her mother.

"Well, what happened?" stammered Millie.

"It's actually unclear what happened. George and another soldier were badly hurt during a firefight in Italy," explained Mrs. Bauer. "They were thought to be dead, but no bodies were recovered, so they sent out the Missing in Action telegram. Finally, they were found, having survived a few weeks in a wooded area. George was near death. They say that if he wasn't in such good physical shape that he would have died."

Millie was blown away. "When did he get back?"

"Do you remember that midnight train?" asked Mrs. Bauer.

Millie nodded.

"He's been at the barracks ever since," said her mother.

Millie was stunned. She replayed the last few months in her head how she and her mother were sneaking around to protect one another. Suddenly, she became angry, thinking back to the day at the barracks when she looked in the window to see her mother and now who she knew was George.

"How could you keep this from me?" She said, lashing out at her mother even though she had been keeping a secret, too.

"We weren't sure if George was even going to make it, Millie," said Mrs. Bauer in a hushed tone. "As you can see, he suffered major burns to his body. He was in a coma for much of his time here. Even now, he is very fragile."

"So, why is he able to come home now?" inquired Millie.

"He was improving," explained Mrs. Bauer. "Do you remember that day that I talked to Mr. Wrigley about you joining the Millerettes?"

Millie shook her head. She recalled how her mother suddenly ran off before they went to go pick out a dress.

Her mother continued. "I was going to surprise you by bringing him home later in the day, but then I got the call that he had a setback and lapsed back into a coma."

Millie sat flabbergasted, mouth agape. Coach came up the stairs and handed her a glass of water.

"We were listening to your game this evening at the barracks," said her mother. "They kept saying your name. Finally, he said. "I want to see Millie.""

"Will he get better?" asked Millie apprehensively, scared that the answer would be no.

"The doctors said he will recover to a certain extent," said Mrs. Bauer, "but with the burns and scarring, he'll never live a completely normal life again."

"Is he home for good?" inquired Millie apprehensively.

"For a few days, but he'll have to return to the hospital for occasional therapies," said her mother.

"Millie," called George from the other room. "I want to see that new glove of yours."

Millie stood up, swallowed hard, and walked into her brother's room.

Epilogue

River Junction Review June 22, 1945

When Coach Shellman's River Junction nine take to the ball diamond for the opening game of their summer campaign tomorrow, they will be led by a young, unproven battery. A pair of soon-to-be sophomores, Millie Bauer will be throwing to Paul Warren when Shellman's squad takes on the Timber Point nine.

"It's no secret that Millie is talented; after all, she is a Bauer," said Shellman. "That Warren kid is the one that caught me by surprise this spring."

Warren, who was tabbed as the team's equipment manager last summer, grew over half a foot since then and showed himself to be the top catcher this spring, taking over for the graduated stalwart, Grogan. According to Shellman, Bauer and Warren have a history of the pitch and catch routine going back to childhood, which should bode well for River Junction.

Millie won't be the only Bauer in uniform for Central High. George Bauer, former stand-out for Central and military hero, joined the coaching staff and will be working with the pitchers. George, who was seriously injured in combat, is recovering nicely. He is attending the River Junction State Teachers College and working at Warren's Grocery & Dry Goods.

About the Author

J.N. Kelly is a lifelong fan of baseball. He spent the summers of his childhood playing on sandlots with his brothers and kids from the neighborhood. He now works as a librarian in Wisconsin, where he lives with his wife and three children. He still dreams about those summer days. Find out more about him here:

www.joeniese.com